# A Winter in Woodstock

Jamie Jones

ISBN: 978-0-578-54570-7

# Dedication

To my husband David, who has cheered me on through any crazy idea I've had over the past 12 years and loved me so well.  I love you, babe.

To our daughter Finley Adelaide, who infuses brain-bending amounts of joy into our lives every moment of every day. You are truly special, hilarious, kind & brilliant. I pray your light never dims.

To my family – ALL of you.  But especially my parents. You're what dreams are made of.

Thank you, God. I am thankful.

# A Note to You

Can I be honest with you?  All I hope you get from this is a lazy afternoon curled up under your favorite blanket. I hope you can visualize every scene like a movie in your head, and I hope you smile more than once.   Last, but not least, I hope you are inspired to visit the enchanting village of Woodstock, Vermont and see just how charming it truly is.

It would mean the world to me if you would leave a review on Amazon. Thank you, and enjoy!

# CHAPTER 1

The leaves on the trees lining the street, once emerald green, had changed into shades of crimson, yellow, orange, and gold. Very soon, they would fall as the season turned from autumn to winter. It was a beautiful and familiar phenomenon for Zoey Larson. In fact, seeing the familiar gleaming of leaves shining like rays of sunshine offered her comfort in the last place she expected to find it.

Downtown Woodstock, Vermont was a picturesque place always ready to serve as a backdrop to some movie requiring a cozy, magically beautiful setting in a charming small town. It was laid back and quaint with

1

close-set businesses in well-kept red-brick buildings with the ubiquitous New England white pillars framing the doorways and porches on most establishments. More than ten years had passed since Zoey lived in Woodstock, but it hadn't changed all that much— and she was glad of that.

The parking lot next to Attorney Pearson's office wasn't full, which was a good sign but didn't lend near as much comfort as the trees and setting did. Zoey parked her rental car and checked her watch. She still had fifteen minutes before she needed to go inside.

Zoey could almost hear Grandma Matilda saying, "You're disappointed; that happens. You know, Zoey, this is your chance to decide if you're the kind of person to pick yourself back up or the kind to wallow. Take a good look all around you—this little corner of the world is shining like rubies. Let's pick ourselves up today and look forward to what comes next."

Bittersweet tears crowded Zoey's eyes at the memory.

Lowering the visor mirror, Zoey added a bit of mascara to her already dark lashes and a touch of pink lipstick to her lips that had turned pale since she last looked in the mirror before her flight.

*I made it through the funeral. I can make it through the reading of the will.* Zoey was second-guessing telling her friend Megan Harris that she didn't need her along for the reading of her grandma's will, especially when she spotted her mother's car in the parking lot.

It was a private reading, which meant her parents likely wouldn't be putting on airs for others. If she went inside, they'd probably start the reading, and perhaps she'd get the painting Grandma Matilda had done during Zoey's senior year of high school. She had so many positive and beautiful memories about Grandma Matilda associated with that painting.

Inhaling deeply through her nose, Zoey looked at herself once more in the visor mirror. *You're a New Yorker, Zoey. You can handle a twenty-minute reading.* Taking the bottle of water from the cupholder, she slipped her arm under her purse strap and exited the rental.

The air was turning colder, but she wore her Albert Nipon long-sleeved, tweed skirt suit she picked up at Neiman Marcus. It was a power suit and had the bonus of being on the warm side. Plus, the light pink and French cream hues were complementary to her fair skin and long, dark brown hair.

Her white heels made crunching sounds as she crossed the gravel parking lot, making her wince as she considered how they would be marked up by the sharp little rocks. The glass door etched with *Attorney Elijah Pearson* pulled outward and the blushing face of Corey Finch—the boy who'd dumped her before the homecoming dance—held the door open for her.

"Zoey, you look amazing. It's so good to see you. Of course, I wish it were under better circumstances," he blustered. "You look great. I'm sorry about your grandma passing on. She was a really cool lady."

"Thanks," Zoey said as she stepped into the lobby. Corey wore a navy-blue suit with a red tie. His hair was still the same auburn from his youth, but his hairline had taken a big step backward. Somehow, that didn't detract from his looks as much as it should have, but maybe that was because men did tend to look distinguished when they were in a suit and tie. "It's nice to see you, too, Corey. Are you here for the reading?"

Corey's eyes swept over her a few times before he answered, "Me? No. I'm a lawyer, an attorney, that is." He cleared his throat, and when he spoke again, his voice was deeper. "Pretty soon it'll say Pearson and Finch on the door."

"That's great. Good for you. That has to make your parents proud."

"Yeah, thanks. I know everyone else is already here. Do you want me to wait out here for whoever you're with and show them in when they get here?"

Zoey shook her head. "I'm on my own today. Is it just back here?" she asked, deciding not to fill him in on her current lack of a social life.

"Yes, I'll walk you back."

Corey offered her his arm, which was much more gentlemanly than he behaved in their youth. He was nice, so she allowed him to lead her down the hall and into a conference room. Zoey first spotted her dad, who was checking his hair in the reflective glass of the window.

The neighbor who lived to the left of Grandma Matilda's bed and breakfast, Mr. Bradshaw, was admiring the framed picture of Grandma Matilda on the small oval table at the far end of the room. Zoey smiled to herself, thinking she'd been right when she'd told Grandma Matilda that Mr. Bradshaw had a crush on her.

*See? I told you, Grandma Matilda.*

"Do you want to sit up by your mom?" Corey asked, angling them both toward the front.

5

"No," Zoey answered, spotting her mother speaking to Elijah Pearson. The attorney was impossible to miss with his black pinstriped suit and broad shoulders. Mr. Pearson, with his olive skin and salt and pepper hair, along with the way he carried himself, could have passed for a movie star. Normally, his prestigious aura would have been enough to magnetize Zoey's mom to him, but she seemed to have a different goal in mind today. No doubt she was trying to find out what she could before the reading of the will. "I'd rather hang back. I have a flight to catch back to New York."

Corey nodded. "Sure."

Zoey pulled out the nearest chair at the main table and sat down. If she was lucky, the reading would begin before either of her parents noticed she had arrived.

Corey made his way to the front of the room where Zoey's mom still spoke with Pearson. Her mom smiled and touched Corey's cheek when he interrupted like he was a puppy there for her amusement. Corey must have been letting Pearson know that everyone had arrived because Pearson moved to the front of the table. "If everyone could take their seats, please. We're going to move ahead with the reading."

Her mom sat next to her dad, which meant their

constant on again off again relationship was going through an on-again swing once more.

*It's not about them. I'm here for Grandma Matilda.*

"Everyone here knew Matilda Dunn Harvey quite well, and so I'm sure it won't surprise any of you that Matilda advised me to keep this short and sweet. In fact, I remember quite clearly when we went over her wishes, Matilda said, 'I know when my time comes it'll be sad, because I know I'm loved and I'll be missed, but this life is for the living, and I want my loved ones to live their best lives, not sit around grieving over me.'"

Zoey blinked back the tears that sprang into her vision and saw Pearson doing the same even though he'd only been her attorney. It didn't surprise Zoey to see him so touched by Grandma Matilda. She was the kind of person who made a loving and lasting impression on practically everyone she ran into.

"In honor of you and your vivaciousness toward life, Matilda, we'll proceed without further ado," Pearson said, addressing Grandma Matilda's picture on the table just behind him. He opened a brown leather-bound folder and lifted it, holding it open in his left hand. "I hope that all of my loved ones are here smiling and celebrating, knowing that I lived a full and happy life. If you're not smiling—you'd better start." Pearson smiled to himself as he read.

"If you're here, you must know that you held a significant and special place in my life and heart. Thank you for coming. Now, let's get to the fun part, which is the part where I get to leave my things to you.

"To my daughter, Marianne Harvey Larson, I leave my mother's diamond earrings, though I know you already have them. I also leave to you and your husband, Derek Larson, your daddy's cabin in Waterbury. I sincerely hope you two can work things out and build a stable relationship with Zoey."

*Nice try, Grandma Matilda.*

"To Marty Bradshaw, I—"

"I'm sorry, I don't mean to interrupt, but does she come back to me later on or is that all she left me?" Mom asked, her right-hand fidgeting with the fake diamonds on her necklace.

"I'm afraid your questions and concerns will have to wait until we've completed the reading," Pearson answered without bothering to hide how distasteful he found her interruption, which Zoey appreciated.

Pearson cleared his throat, fixing her mom with a hard look that encouraged her to keep her mouth shut.

"To Marty Bradshaw, I leave my recipe for my famous Norwegian Potato Crepes you loved so much, both of my late husband's Civil War rifles, and my book on gardening, because you and I both know your rose bushes need more love than they're getting."

Mr. Bradshaw laughed with his arms still folded tightly at his chest.

"To Maybell Higgins, I leave all of my stained-glass tools and supplies. You know you were always better at it than I was. I also leave you my Tracker off-roading ATV, because I know how you like to get out and explore. Keep exploring, Maybell, I've always loved your adventurous spirit."

Maybell smiled slightly and then hid her face in her handkerchief, crying quietly. Her blond and silver-streaked hair was pulled into a loose French twist.

Zoey scooted over two seats so she could put her arm around Maybell, who was always one of Grandma Matilda's best friends. She missed the next few things that were given by her grandma as she tried to offer Maybell comfort.

Grandma Matilda gave money to several charities and the church she sometimes attended, and then Pearson turned his attention to Zoey. She braced herself, not wanting to cry— if she started, it would be tough to stop.

"To my granddaughter, who was like a daughter to me, and very best friend as well…"

Zoey swallowed hard and bit the inside of her cheek to keep from tearing up again when so many eyes were on her.

"… I leave the entirety of everything else I possessed in this lifetime, which includes the bed and breakfast, the Range Rover, my pictures, computers, remaining savings, the canoes, camper, and everything inside of the bed and breakfast that was not already listed and given to someone else in this reading. It was my greatest honor to be in your life in any capacity, my dear Zoey. Don't you be sad. Remember we always pick ourselves back up, because that's who we are. I know you're going to make the bed and breakfast an even greater success."

Zoey tasted blood and realized she was biting too hard, frozen in shock.

*Did he say the bed and breakfast?*

"I'm sorry, Mr. Pearson, I know you said not to interrupt, but are you sure you read that correctly? She couldn't have left the inn to me. Not to me. She knew I established myself in New York; my life is in New York."

*Shut up. Close your mouth.*

Zoey laughed nervously, feeling the heat rising in her cheeks as everyone in the room looked at her. She unbuttoned the tweed blazer and took a deep breath, trying to compose herself. "I'm a writer, a news writer, not a businesswoman. I don't think…"

"I went over the details with Matilda very carefully, and she told me more than once that she wanted you to have and run her inn after she passed. I know it seems like a lot, but she was sure insistent that it was for you. Take some time and just let it settle. I know your grandma's passing was unexpected for you and is still so fresh. Give it some time."

Zoey nodded absently as Grandma Matilda's words repeated in her mind, "I know you're going to make the bed and breakfast an even greater success."

*I live in New York. I can't run an inn in Vermont! Grandma Matilda, what am I going to do?*

# CHAPTER 2

"You're still stressing about it, I can tell." Megan, Zoey's friend and coworker, pointed her stylus pen at Zoey. "Just sell the inn if you don't want it."

Zoey clicked send on her laptop, turning in the last article she needed to write for the next three weeks. "It's not that easy, Megan. My grandma loved that place. Last year, she built an addition so she could book more guests, even though I begged her not to work too hard. There wasn't a single conversation I had with her since I moved to New York that didn't involve how much she loves… I mean, how much she loved the place."

"But she'd want you to be happy."

"You didn't hear what she wrote to me for the reading of the will. She wanted me to have it and run it. I can't just sell it."

Megan shrugged. "You're just gonna give up your career here? Just in case you've forgotten, sweetie, it took a two-year internship before they even considered hiring you on."

"I know." Zoey covered her face with both hands. "I've got to go and sort through her belongings, so I'll figure out what to do then."

"You said that after the reading, and that was almost a month ago."

Zoey dropped her hands from her face to give Megan a look that let her know she was no longer being helpful.

"Everyone, wrap up what you're doing and meet in the conference room in ten," Kenzie's secretary, Celeste, announced over the intercom.

Megan sipped her coffee and started typing furiously, which gave Zoey the chance to slip away and hopefully end the good-intentioned nagging coming her way. She shut down her computer and went to the office kitchen to refill her water bottle.

Jake Ward was already in the kitchen, polishing off

half of what looked like a peanut butter and jelly sandwich. Jake was a journalist as well, though he tended to be most interested in reporting weather and geological phenomena. Zoey didn't know him all that well, even though they'd worked at the same place for nearly a year. She buried herself in her work, but she wasn't blind.

Jake was a handsome, friendly guy with a carefree spirit about him. He was your typical creative type—not too athletic, nose always in a book, and as outgoing as anyone you'd ever meet.

"I got another half sandwich if you want it," Jake offered with a welcoming smile.

"That's okay. My luck, I'd get a big glob of peanut butter somewhere and wear it into the meeting," Zoey said as she reminded herself that even if Megan was nagging, she was right.

Jake was still smiling when she turned back after refilling the water bottle. "What's funny?"

"There's a smudge of something on your cheek."

*Of course, there is.*

"Jake, you can't just smile at a person who's all marked up. Help me," Zoey said, handing him a napkin.

"It looks like ink from reading the newspaper. You

know it's practically a paperless world now, don't you?" he said with that light of amusement ever-present in his bright green eyes.

Zoey felt a blush building and took the napkin from him once he wiped it gently over her right cheek. "Speaking of the news, you're writing the weather, and I've got a weather question. I might fly out to Vermont this weekend. Do you have any weather warnings for me?"

"Vermont? Whereabouts?"

"I'd be flying into Rutland Vermont Regional but headed to Woodstock. I know there's going to be snow, it's Christmas— but I mean winter storms and unfriendly flying weather."

Jake nodded. "Yeah, there's a big storm due in that region this weekend, but I predicted the storm hitting Saturday night. You have a little time to get there ahead of the storm. When are you leaving?"

Zoey tried to keep her calm. "Well, I… I'm not sure. I don't know how much I want to fly into that little airport when there's a big storm coming." Zoey tugged open the top button on her blouse to try and free herself of that strangling sensation she tended to feel whenever she let worry and anxiety stomp through her system.

"There's a meeting, you two. Remember?" Megan poked her fire-red head of hair into the kitchen. "Unless you two need some—"

Knowing her friend was going to embarrass her, Zoey cut her off, "We're coming right now, office enforcer."

"Oh, wait." Jake took the napkin from Zoey's hand. "You missed a spot."

Zoey looked at Megan so that she wouldn't be looking at Jake with big apprehensive eyes. It was getting ridiculous how often she avoided having any glimmer of romance in her life. Truth be told, Zoey would be breaking new ground to do something social that wasn't work-related.

Megan wiggled her red brows at Zoey and made herself scarce.

*And she's off making this into something it's definitely not. Great.*

"Thanks."

"You could drive up and skip the plane ride."

Zoey nodded gratefully when Jake stepped back and didn't mention just how deeply she was blushing. That was kind of him, and somehow, that just made her blush harder.

"I don't have a car, but I could just rent one."

"I'd offer to drive you, but I don't want to crash your Christmas celebration plans. I really wouldn't mind, though. It would be great to get some footage and pics to go with my weather report."

Zoey and Jake were almost out of the kitchen when he made his offer. She wasn't sure if it would be a good idea to bring him, since she hadn't planned on doing any Christmas celebrating. Zoey expected to spend the holiday sorting through her grandma's things and figuring out what to do with the inn and didn't want to put a damper on his Christmas.

"You wouldn't rather spend Christmas with your family?" she asked, selfishly hoping he wouldn't.

"My family is spending Christmas overseas this year. I don't have anything better to do if you want a road trip companion."

"She does," Megan answered for her as soon as they exited the kitchen. "Thanks, Jake."

Celeste opened the conference room door and waved at the three impatiently to join the meeting, so Zoey didn't get to confirm that she would like to have him come along. It would be great to have someone around to keep her from wallowing in how much she

17

missed Grandma and to remind her of everything she'd worked for in New York.

"Now that we're all here..." Kenzie Highsmith, Editor-in-Chief of Birdseye Publishing, signaled the three to take their seats. "We've got great material set to publish while we are away for the holiday for the next two weeks, but that doesn't mean I want you to put your journalist brains to sleep. We'll need some catchy, intriguing, and captivating pieces for the new year."

Celeste nodded along, as usual, acting as though she were just as important as the Editor-in-Chief.

"Send in your articles, ideas, and images. Wow me, people. Being a journalist isn't a lazy career, and the news never sleeps. We have the interns pulling the heavy weight during the holiday, so it isn't like we'll be truly closed. Celeste will be in the office ready to relay and proof anything you might have."

Everyone in the meeting sat on the edge of their seats, scribbling notes or leaning forward as if ready to launch from their chairs to find the next big story — everyone except for Jake.

"You all remember how you got your jobs. Your articles outshined another journalist, and you took their seat. Let's keep that in mind as your understudies run things here. Yes? Right, Zoey?" Kenzie focused her cut-throat gaze on Zoey.

"Absolutely," Zoey said, doing her best to appear confident and on top of her life when she felt the complete opposite.

Jake resealed the Ziploc bag that held the remainder of his sandwich, and the crinkling sound stole the focus of both Kenzie and the rest of the meeting occupants.

"Something to add, Jake?" Kenzie asked, raising her thin dark eyebrows.

"Nope. I couldn't agree more. Zoey and I were just having a similar conversation. I'm getting some great ideas for my article this weekend, and Zoey has an idea for a Christmas festival piece based in Vermont."

Kenzie turned her shrewd gaze back to Zoey. "I'm glad you're going to make use of the time off, especially since you requested an additional week. You had me worried."

Zoey forced a smile that she hoped would project reassurance and confidence.

"I look forward to seeing what you come up with," Kenzie said, making Zoey quite sure she hadn't pulled off the smile she was shooting for.

Luckily, she turned her attention to the other side of

the room after that, so Zoey could do some slow breathing and avoid looking frazzled.

"So? What do you say? You up for a road trip?" Jake asked, leaning toward Zoey.

"Oh, yeah, it's set in stone now. We're going."

He snickered, which made Zoey tense up again because she did not want to regain Kenzie's attention. "When do you want to head out?"

"Tomorrow morning work for you?" Zoey asked.

Megan grinned at Zoey from the other side of Jake, failing to be inconspicuous with her feelings.

"Text me your address, and I'll pick you up at ten."

*Ten? That's almost noon, isn't it? Oh, who cares, at least I'm committed to going and getting this done.*

Jake passed Zoey a yellow Post-it note with his name scrawled beneath his number and what looked like a maze or masked face doodled next to it. She must have given her puzzlement away, because Jake said, "It's a snowflake," with a laugh once the meeting ended.

"Oh, yeah. I know," Zoey lied before tucking the Post-it into the pocket of her suit jacket. "See you tomorrow."

# CHAPTER 3

The tower of luggage Zoey erected threatened to topple when the trio on the second floor insisted on squeezing into the already packed elevator. Zoey used her body and the back wall to keep the luggage from tumbling down. Someone commented on how they'd keep whatever bag fell into their arms if Zoey didn't win the balancing battle.

That probably was not the reason why there were so many shoves and pushes against Zoey and her luggage. More likely, people were just in a hurry and didn't intend to get stuck behind Zoey as she attempted to drive the luggage tower.

She tipped the tower toward her, gripping the handle on the powder blue suitcase with wheels on the bottom. Once she had it at an angle, Zoey reached and pushed the indigo jean duffle bag on top to secure it. She pulled the luggage as she backed out of the elevator and squeezed past the people who boarded from the lobby.

"Holiday travel is a nightmare," she muttered to herself, but she was glad that she managed to keep her luggage intact. Zoey drove her luggage through the entryway of the apartment building. She used the side ramp meant for wheelchairs, avoiding the stairs, and was done with all the bother of travel by the time she parked her luggage on the wet, salty sidewalk.

Jake wasn't there yet, which she knew since she'd left her apartment before he called her with his ETA. Zoey didn't want to keep him waiting, so she wheeled her luggage outside. Once out on the sidewalk, however, she wondered if she should have waited in the entryway instead. The sidewalk was busy—too busy to let go of the bags to get her gloves on. Her breath expelled in big foggy puffs as Zoey tried to stay out of the way of the traffic.

"Need a ride, pretty lady?" The male voice coming from behind made her jump. Zoey turned to tell the man to get lost, before realizing it was Jake.

"I thought you were going to call first," Zoey said, eyeing his dark purple beanie and wishing she'd grabbed her own hat. His black hair poked out from under the brim in soft, short, wayward curls that intrigued Zoey, since his hair was usually straight.

Jake took the two duffle bags from the heap and led the way to his white Mitsubishi Outlander. "I thought I'd get here and call, but when I arrived, you were already outside in this winter freeze."

"Yeah, I should've checked the weather. I thought we'd have more time before the blizzard came through, but the sky looks pretty ominous."

"Rub it in," Jake laughed as he hefted the last piece of her luggage into his trunk. "Predicting the weather is a best guess based on science."

Zoey nodded in agreement but was far too cold to join in his laughter. Jake must have noticed because he opened the passenger side door for her and left it open as he circled to the driver's side. Zoey slipped into the passenger seat—shutting the door and blocking the cold air.

The car was already toasty warm, and Zoey could have cried with relief as her toes began to defrost. It was her own fault really; she should have worn more sensible shoes, but she got rid of her more comfortable clothing when she moved into her city apartment because she worked crazy hours and couldn't afford to look unprofessional.

"It's going to be worse traffic than usual," Jake said as he negotiated his way into the flow of traffic.

"Yeah, maybe we should fly after all. I didn't mean to rope you into a super long road trip."

Jake laughed. "Rope me in? I'm pretty sure between me and Megan you didn't really have a choice. Besides, you're right about that ominous sky. It's about to dump snow like crazy. All the flights for the next six hours are grounded, and I bet they'll extend that timeframe to twelve hours at least."

Zoey took another look at the thick clouds above the New York skyline and nodded. "I'd be grounded and waiting if you weren't driving, so thank you."

"You sure you want to thank me? I volunteered you for an additional article yesterday in that meeting. I can help you with it if you like. I'd hate to make you miss out on time with your family during the holiday. I was trying to get that fire-breather off your back."

"No worries. I think it'll be good for me to have the

article to work on. I'm not going to Woodstock to visit with family, anyway."

Jake made a sound of astonishment before he took the turnoff to merge onto the freeway heading north. "I'm so rude. I didn't even ask you what you were going to be doing in Woodstock. I got too caught up in the excitement of observing the blizzard that I forgot to ask."

"There's nothing wrong with being passionate about your work," Zoey said.

"I heard you say once that you were from Woodstock, so I just assumed."

Zoey nodded, wondering when he'd heard her say that. He had a good memory, and she already knew he had a sharp mind. "I am. My Grandma Matilda raised me in Woodstock. She's the one I went to visit when I traveled back earlier this year. She passed away early last month."

Jake's green eyes filled with empathy as he listened. "She must have been one heck of a lady. She did a great job of raising you. I bet she was so proud of you."

Without giving it any forethought, words just started spilling out of Zoey. "I really did think she was, but then she went and left me her inn in Woodstock. In her will, she made a statement that I would make it an even greater success than it already was. That doesn't sound like she wanted me to hire someone else to run it, does it?"

Jake wrinkled his nose a little. "No, it doesn't sound like she did."

"Exactly. I know she wouldn't want me to sell it, not after all the hard work she put into it over the years. But why did she pick *me*? My mom was chomping at the bit before and even during the reading of the will. I know she told Grandma Matilda that she wanted it. I never said that I did."

"You and your grandma were close though, weren't you?"

Zoey sighed. "We were. She knew about all my long hours interning to get on fulltime with Birdseye Publishing. Grandma Matilda encouraged me when I told her about pursuing writing and journalism. She was there every step of the way. That's why I don't get it."

"I wish I could tell you what she was thinking. This will be my first trip out to Woodstock. It's pretty cool we're going to an inn, and we don't have to make reservations though, right?"

"Sunny-side up kind of guy, aren't you, Jake? Man,

my Grandma Matilda would've loved you. I mean, she loved everyone, but you two would've been on the same page about a lot, I think."

Jake grinned, and Zoey sat closer than she usually dared since they weren't at work. She noticed he had a slight dimple on both cheeks.

"So, your Grandma Matilda was a positive, hardworking, brutishly handsome woman, with an eye for detail and a love of exploring?"

"I wouldn't describe her as brutishly handsome, but the rest sounds about right." Zoey smiled, realizing that somehow Jake made it easy to talk about the woman she loved and missed so much. "She had a way of looking at situations and people with this sort of knowing and understanding. I would've loved to inherit that gift."

Jake glanced her way with his handsome smile still in place. "I thought that was women's intuition?"

"If it is, I got robbed," Zoey laughed.

"You must have inherited your sensible disposition from your father then, since I don't see you as the type to chomp at the bit at a will reading."

Smoothing her hands over her black and white checkered leggings, she shook her head. "I'm not, but I don't think my dad gave me the talent of being prudent.

He isn't very sensible. My parents are both quite different than me. My grandma said that I reminded her of my grandfather, who passed away while I was still young. I don't remember him very well, unfortunately."

"Your Grandma Matilda didn't talk about him very much? Did her new husband get jealous?"

"No. She never remarried. I think she didn't talk about him very often because she still missed him so much."

Jake sighed a lonesome sound. "Matilda sounds like she was a true romantic."

Zoey never thought about it that way before, but he was right. "She was."

"So, you'll be deciding what to do with the inn, and I went and threw a Christmas article on top of all that? You've got to let me help you with it. At least let me get the pictures."

"Yeah, actually that would be great if you really don't mind."

Jake relaxed a bit against the seat. "It's the least I can do. I enjoy getting footage, so really I'm just being greedy."

"Yeah, yeah. You're really kind, and I appreciate it. I'll be going through the inn and the things she left me as well. I've been putting it off, and you coming with me is making me think that I might be able to get through it."

"Will your parents not be there or are they away for the holidays?"

Zoey shrugged. "I really don't know. I'm not close to either of them. Grandma Matilda was always the one who was there for me. My parents might pass through, but I hope they don't. I haven't told them I'll be in Woodstock. That doesn't mean they won't hear about my being there—it's such a small town."

"The rumor mill is healthy, I'm sure. They usually are in small towns. Will it be an issue if I'm staying at the inn with you? I don't want to sully your pristine reputation."

"Pristine," Zoey repeated, rolling her eyes. "I doubt it. There will be curious people and questions, but they'd be there whether you came with me or not."

Jake smiled as the lanes began to open up. "The snow is coming down and thinning out the crowds. We may end up being the only crazies driving in this mess." He laughed. "Don't worry, I've got all-wheel drive, and I drive like a grandpa."

"I appreciate that, but if it gets too bad, we can pull off and get a hotel room or something."

The snort that came out of Jake had Zoey laughing again, and she forgot to remain worried about the roads. "What was that?"

"That's me saying no thanks to the Christmas season rates at the hotels."

Zoey bit her lower lip and smoothed her hair over her right shoulder. "You make a valid point."

"We'll take it slow. So, you were saying you don't think your parents will be dropping by?"

*Parents in title only, and that's the truth.*

"I imagine they'll remain in Waterbury at the cabin they got in the will. It belonged to my grandfather. With the impending storm, I doubt they'll make the drive to Woodstock. Regardless, I'm sure we'll be quite busy with all the work we need to get done."

"Tell you what, you bribe me with some hot chocolate, and I'll be happy to crack the work whip at you."

"Uh oh, you seem a little too eager about that whip cracking, Jake."

He played with an imaginary mustache, probably thinking he looked like some evil genius in a cartoon. He didn't even come close to looking creepy or sinister, which made it easier to laugh at his attempt.

"I did drive a team of sled dogs in Alaska. I didn't go farther than a few blocks and may have only whipped the snow, but I've swung a whip before."

"You have to tell me about Alaska," Zoey said, turning in her seat toward him again. He was so easy to talk with. It was a shame she hadn't taken the time to get to know him sooner.

# CHAPTER 4

"This is where I want to get married," Zoey said as Grandma Matilda draped the soft white fur blanket around her shoulders.

Snowflakes glistened in the sunlight as they fell from the sky, making Grandma Matilda's smile look magical as she gazed at Zoey. She was hanging more white lights along the aisle for the winter wedding. "You've got a lot to do before you need to worry about getting married, Zoey. But I have to say—I'd really love it if you got married here."

The white gazebo was decked in green garland, lights, and red ribbon. The evergreen trees and bushes *were getting frosted with the falling snow, and the contrasting shades made the whites seem whiter and the greens even deeper and lush.*

*"Your friend Tabitha is coming over. Go see if she's here yet," Grandma Matilda said as she continued to work.*

*Zoey ran down the path between the rows of wooden benches and up the steps onto the wraparound porch pretending she was a snow princess with a fur cape. The porch swing swayed with a man and woman who were staying at the inn. They were sitting close to one another with a look of peace and happiness. The man was watching the flames in the outdoor fireplace while the woman was gazing at the Christmas and wedding décor.*

*The white floorboards of the porch had a spring to them that Zoey was certain grown-ups didn't know about because they would bounce a lot more on the porch if they did. Every window she raced by had a planter beneath it with red and white poinsettias, pinecones, red berries, and big green leaves.*

*There were two pairs of adults playing chess she nearly crashed into but managed to avoid.*

*"We're all booked up," she remembered Grandma*

*Matilda saying as she dodged another group near the front of the house. They were talking about going to see the Christmas celebration in Woodstock or staying in and watching the wedding.*

*Tabitha met her at the front door, and they moved away from the chilly air into the warm house that smelled like maple and cinnamon. The hardwood floors were polished, and the rugs had intricate designs woven in them.*

*Because Tabitha was still warming up, they set up a tea party with their dolls in front of the mantle with the fire going. The mantle had tall nutcrackers standing on each end, which Zoey informed Tabitha were really soldiers guarding the castle.*

*They played tea party, eating cookies from the oversized kitchen and chocolate milk as their tea. After they ate the cookies and depleted their supply of chocolate milk, they pretended that the crystal chandelier with all its hanging drops of rainbow magic crystals was a falling star.*

*"I wish I could grow up and be just like my Grandma Matilda," Zoey said. "I want every day to be just like this one."*

*Tabitha started to make a wish, but she took so long*

*that Zoey fell asleep. When she woke, it was a summer day, and she and Tabitha were playing hide and seek in the garden.*

*Zoey was looking for Tabitha and trying not to touch too much since her fingers were still sticky with watermelon juice. The brick-paved pathways were seamless and warm under her bare feet.*

*She forgot she was looking for Tabitha as soon as she noticed Grandma Matilda on the extra-tall ladder straightening the weathervane on top of one of the two spires of the house. She looked like an angel hanging a star with the sun at her back. The dark black shingles on the roof looked like a slide to Zoey, but Grandma Matilda made her promise to stay off the roof.*

*Tabitha got tired of hiding and came out of her hiding place under one of the carved stone benches surrounded on two sides by huge pink and yellow rose bushes full of sweetly perfumed blooms. The green grass on the lawn felt cool and soft under her feet as she and Tabitha raced around playing tag.*

*After they ran until they were breathless, they went into the house and drank raspberry lemonade in the library. Zoey's favorite place to sit was the window seat with the thick cushion that was like a plush flower-*

*patterned bed. There were so many books on so many different topics. The polished wood furniture was shiny, smelling of lemon and orange. The curtains at the window were usually open but draped to each side, reminding Zoey of a magical doorway into what had to be a fairy paradise.*

*Tabitha found an animal encyclopedia and the two girls hefted the big book onto the roll-top desk. It was so well polished the book nearly slipped off the other side. They looked at lizards through the huge magnifying glass that belonged to grandpa.*

The sensation of falling shot butterflies through Zoey's stomach, and she sat up, startled.

"Whoa, I didn't see that speed bump with all the snow." Jake put his hand on her shoulder. "You good?"

"Yeah, yeah. I'm good. I didn't mean to fall asleep. How long have I been out?" Zoey asked, trying to wipe her mouth discretely in case she'd been drooling.

Jake gave her one of his easy, handsome smiles. "Only a couple hours or so."

"Or so? I'm sorry, I didn't even take a turn driving."

"You can now if it'll make you feel better, but I think I passed the sign for Woodstock a little way back."

Zoey laughed, shaking her head. "I'll have to make you some hot chocolate at least."

"Yeah, I'll take you up on that. You said Highland Avenue, right?"

Zoey recognized the bank on the right-hand side of the road even though it was covered in snow. "Yes. I'll guide you. Just keep going straight. This is the main road in Woodstock."

"Is it? Wow, this is a small town. There's the Yankee Bookshop; I'll have to come back tomorrow when they're open."

Zoey nodded and then pointed a little farther up the street to the Mon Vert Café with its bright blue canopies decked with Christmas lights. "That's where you'll want to go first tomorrow. Mon Vert Café is the place to go if you want good food. I'll do some cooking if I have time, but I don't think there's going to be much in the inn as far as fresh groceries. I'll have to make a run to the market, too. I bet they're open even with this blizzard."

"Really? It's coming down pretty thick."

Zoey nodded in agreement. "Take the next right

onto Lincoln Street and then bear right at the split onto Mountain Peg Road."

"I can't see the street signs in all this mess, just tell me when to turn."

Jake gave her a few funny looks as she guided him through the near U-turn onto Mountain Peg Road. The streets were a bit winding but appeared to have been freshly plowed.

The Snapdragon Inn—Grandma Matilda's inn— was buried in snow, and so it was lucky Jake's car had all-wheel drive. It wasn't quite dark yet, but with the heavy snowfall coming down so thick, it might as well have been. Jake parked as close as he could to the front door.

Zoey dug out her keys and stared at the dark porch that she couldn't ever remember appearing so dim.

*It must be because Grandma Matilda isn't here to welcome us inside.*

"I'll unlock the door." Zoey pushed the car door open and waded through the deep snow that came up to the tops of her knees in her poorly selected leggings. Teeth chattering, she dusted the snow from the lock and inserted the key as she noticed the glass on the window was cracked but not broken. The door groaned as it opened, revealing the unlit foyer. The air was stale and carried the same dust that powdered the hardwood floors.

Zoey flipped the light switch, illuminating the entryway around her. She turned on the next switch for the outside lights.

"This is a gorgeous house, Zoey," Jake said as he climbed the porch stairs carrying one of her duffle bags and one of his. "I don't know why I had it in my head when you said it was your Grandma Matilda's place it would be smaller."

"Yeah, it's big… and it looks like it requires some dusting."

"Dusting is easy." Jake set the bags down as he admired the staircase.

*He's right. It just needs some cleaning, and it'll be just like I remembered it.*

"I'll get the heat going and maybe a fire on. You don't have to bring in my bags, I'll get the rest of them," Zoey said, glad once again that she wasn't facing the Snapdragon Inn with all the memories it held alone.

# CHAPTER 5

Rays of gold and white reached through the crack in the curtains, waking Zoey from more dreams of her cherished childhood memories at the inn with Grandma Matilda. For an instant, when she opened her eyes and saw the familiar ivory curtains with eyelet detail and the cheerful yellow-gold walls, she thought to call out to Grandma Matilda and reassure her that she was up and awake.

As she blinked the sleep from her eyes, she noticed the way the ivory curtains were yellowing, and the bright yellow-gold painted walls were fading. The shabby state of the room reminded her that Grandma Matilda had passed away from the cancer that came upon her and extinguished the brightest burning life Zoey had ever been around.

"I really should have made time to come home more, Grandma Matilda. I didn't realize you were struggling to keep up with the dusting and vacuuming. At least I could've hired someone to help you."

*And now I'm talking to myself — nothing like home to make you lose your marbles a little bit.*

Zoey didn't have to check the clock to confirm the time. She'd been on a strict schedule for years, waking at six in the morning every day. Of course, even though she didn't have to look at the clock to confirm the time, she did.

Six-fifteen.

*What do you know? I slept in a little.*

Each suite had a private bathroom attached to it, and Zoey made use of the shower. A few of the tiles had fallen off, and the handle on the bathroom sink controlling the cold water came off in her hand.

"I thought you secured a loan to expand and fix up this place?" she said as if speaking to her grandmother.

After dressing, she headed to the kitchen to see what she could scrounge up for breakfast. In each hallway, she found loose boards, cracked paint on the walls, faded material, scuff marks on the floors, holes in the faded rugs—the list went on and on.

"Good morning, how did you sleep?" Jake asked her once she reached the kitchen.

"Oh, no, I meant to beat you down here, but I got distracted. There are quite a few things that need repairing around here."

"I know, I could hear you in the upper hallway fighting with that loose board." Jake chuckled.

"I'm sorry. Did I wake you?"

"I was already up and showered by then."

Jake was wearing a navy-blue beanie, with an olive-green cable-knit sweater and dark blue jeans. He smelled like sweet apples, no doubt the scent of the shampoo and conditioner in the room Grandma Matilda dubbed Suite Apple Pie. The curls of his black hair looked like they might still be wet where they peeked from beneath the beanie.

"Your hair is always straight at work," she observed aloud.

"Is it?" His grin grew, exposing his straight white teeth. He looked like an upgraded version of the Bounty Man from the paper towel commercials.

Zoey nodded and opened the pantry. "I can't see you as the type to flat iron your hair, but I could be wrong."

"No, you're right. I comb some gel through it until it straightens out."

"It looks nice curly, too," Zoey said, feeling that telltale blush of hers igniting in her cheeks. "We've lots of canned food and baking mix."

Jake nodded. "The fridge had some stuff in it but most of it I had to throw out. There are still some good condiments."

"I'll make a run to the market. I'll be quick."

"I'd like to come with you, if you don't mind. It was too dark last night to get a good look at the town."

Zoey nodded. "It was. I feel bad it was such a long drive. It was only supposed to be about four and a half hours and ended up being… what six?"

Jake just grinned back, which meant it'd probably taken even more than six. "If you want to drive, you can."

"I do. But let's take the Range Rover my Grandma Matilda left me." The keys to the Range Rover were on the hook next to the front door, and Zoey paused when she saw the beads on the keychain she'd tied on a string for Grandma Matilda when she was just a girl.

"Do you mind if we swing by that café you mentioned last night for some coffee?"

Jake's question rescued Zoey from tearing up at the bittersweet memory. "That sounds good to me."

Inside the garage, there was a woodworking table that was once used by Zoey's grandpa—at least that was what Grandma Matilda told her. An impressive collection of tools hung on the pegboard and probably more were stored in the toolboxes. Zoey eyed the pegboard, making a mental note of what tools she had on hand so when they returned, she might be able to fix some of the things that'd fallen into disrepair.

The dark gray Range Rover was clean and smelled like cucumber-melon, Grandma Matilda's favorite scent. Zoey pushed the button for the garage door, and it opened, albeit with a lot of bouncing as if it was suffering from a bout of hiccups. The engine fired right up, which was a relief.

Once Zoey backed the car out of the garage, she waited while the garage door hiccupped its way to the closed position. In the light of day, the house showed more wear than it had appeared to when they arrived in the late evening. The bright seafoam-green siding had once been vibrant but was now darkened and faded, giving the house a dull and aged appearance.

The hardwood floor on the wraparound porch looked like it had buckled in a few places, and the beautiful seating areas she remembered were all but gone. "Sorry," Zoey said, realizing she was staring at the house while Jake patiently waited. "It's just so different than I remember."

"That's understandable; it was your childhood home," Jake said.

"True, but I came back a few times over the past ten years, and I never noticed the need for repairs. I wish I'd paid better attention."

Jake took his camera out of the bag on his shoulder. "I'm sure that had a lot to do with the fact that you were getting to visit with your grandma."

"Yes, I'm sure that's it. She had such a warm presence, and of course, she didn't want me to worry, so she wouldn't have told me."

Zoey drove down the long, curved driveway to the street. It was nice seeing the neighboring houses in daylight. Mr. Bradshaw's yellow and white house looked much the same as she remembered it, nestled away from the street in the thick forest. Although, it appeared he'd expanded on his wood carving hobby, as there was a family of wooden bears near the front of his house.

When she turned onto Lincoln, she couldn't help but notice how excited Jake became as they passed the different homes. "It's a cute little town," she commented.

"There's so much space and each home looks like they've got their own little paradise. I don't know why you ever wanted to leave this place."

Taking a left onto Stanton Street, she chuckled. "When you put it that way, I don't know why I did either. Just getting in and out of the elevator at my apartment building yesterday made me jealous of how much space sardines in a can get to themselves."

"Look, you can see the river between those two buildings," Jake said, raising his camera.

"That's the Ottauquechee River, but the locals call it the Quechee River. It runs right through town. I can get you a better view of it than this." Zoey made another left onto Pleasant Street. It had been plowed, and the sidewalks already shoveled. People were out and about despite the deep snow, walking their dogs and visiting with one another as though they were in no particular hurry to reach their destinations.

Jake leaned forward in his seat as Zoey parked the

car. He read the sign aloud. "Mac's Woodstock Market." His smile made Zoey laugh again as he reminded her of an excited child about to get on an amusement park ride.

It was still early enough in the day that the market wasn't too busy. The shelves were well-stocked, and Mac's Market had the staples Zoey and Jake had been looking for.

They split up to do some personal item shopping. Zoey picked up a couple of packages of light bulbs, and some Liquid Nails so she could fix the tiles in the bathroom. When she found Jake once more, he held a bag of mini marshmallows and was discussing with Mrs. Billings—one of the biggest gossips in town—the necessity for whipped cream on hot chocolate.

"There you are, Zoey. Look at you all grown up. I know everyone is going to be so thrilled to hear you're back and running the Snapdragon Inn. It's one of a kind, and it'd be a shame to let it fall into the hands of strangers."

"Well, I haven't made up my mind about what I'm going to do with it yet. But it was nice to see you, Mrs. Billings."

Jake added the mini marshmallows to the basket on top of the tins of hot chocolate. "Nice to meet you," he said to Mrs. Billings.

"You've got a very nice young man, Zoey. Good for you."

Zoey felt her face burning with a blush as she shook her head. "No, we're not together. We're just coworkers and friends. He's a journalist, too, and he's writing a piece on Woodstock. Maybe you'll be in it," Zoey said, hoping to change the trajectory of the gossip toward the article and not the relationship she had with Jake.

Mrs. Billings smiled brighter and tested the bounce of her silver and red curls with her hand. "That's lovely. How interesting."

"Thank you. I'll be in touch if there's something I can ask of you for the article." Jake smiled. "Ready to go?"

"Sure." Zoey held in her laugh at his obvious discomfort.

Jake hooked his arm through hers and hurried their walk up to the cash register. "You know she's going to be showing up during every photoshoot I do in this town now, don't you?"

"Better she focuses on your feature than trying to make people think we're an item, trust me."

"Shameless," Jake said, laughing.

Zoey insisted on buying the groceries, and once they were loaded into the car, they drove to the Mon Vert Café and purchased hot coffee and coffee beans to take back to the inn. To make it up to Jake for siccing Mrs. Billings on him, she drove to Middle Covered Bridge so he could get some good shots of the Quechee River.

The covered bridge was alight with gold Christmas lights, and an oversized green wreath with a big red bow hung on the entrance face above the opening.

"Look at the view," Jake said as he slid out of the Range Rover. "The mountains, forest, and river are so big it makes Woodstock feel so small and quaint. It's such a beautiful place to call home. I'm envious you got to grow up here."

It was impossible to disagree with him, especially when she joined him at the railing near the entrance of the walkway where he took pictures of the landscape and river. The rushing sound of the water and the soothing sway of the trees with the light breeze made the stress and sadness Zoey had been carrying ease and nearly drift away completely.

She didn't even notice when Jake walked farther up the street to take pictures of her standing just outside the walkway, which was illuminated in golden light.

When she spotted him, she gave an embarrassed laugh, wondering what she looked like as she stared at the rushing water wishing to float away rather than make such a hard decision.

"I assume you've snapped what you wanted of the water," she said, shaking her head. "I'm going to head back and put some time into the inn. Hop in, and I'll give you a lift to your car so you can go explore and take more interesting pictures than those of me getting my hair messed up in this wind."

"You couldn't look messed up. Even with your hair on the fluffier side, you still look all polished and professional. I don't know how you do it."

They got into the car and drove to the inn. Along the drive, Zoey noticed that the townspeople who were out were paying more attention to them as they drove by than they had before.

*Clearly, the town gossip mill is alive and well.*

"I can take the stuff in if you want to head back out," Zoey offered as they watched the garage door stutter its way open.

"Well, we've got another wave of snow coming in this afternoon. I think I'm going to wait and see if I can

50

get some pictures right before or right as it's dropping. You should let me give you a hand with your house projects. I know a little plumbing."

Zoey pulled into the garage, waiting for what else he might offer. When he didn't proceed to list any further skills, she turned off the car and winced. "Is there an issue with the plumbing?"

"Oh, sorry, I thought you might've seen the bathroom in the room across from mine. I went in there last night to use the sink since the one in my room isn't draining, but it's dismantled, and the shower is, too."

"Yes. You're helping me with the plumbing," Zoey answered right away. "I mean, please? I have no idea how to reassemble a sink or a shower."

Jake reached across and squeezed her shoulder. "No problem. Don't worry. I will help you with the shower and the sinks."

"You're a saint, Jake."

They unloaded the groceries and raided her grandpa's tools for wrenches and the like so Jake could get started on the plumbing. He promised to call out to her if he needed help, so Zoey got her pen and paper and began making a list of necessary repairs, going from room to room.

When she opened the front door to take a closer look at the porch, there was a whole slew of women just climbing the steps.

*Oh, crap. What's going on?*

"… I'm just saying we should have called first," Gertrude McMillan—known for her fear of everything—complained as she was pulled up the stairs. Maybell Higgins was doing the pulling, utterly ignoring Gertrude's complaints as her curly blond and silver-streaked ponytail swished from side to side.

"Zoey." Maybell grinned, releasing Gertrude to rush forward and hug Zoey. "It is so good to see you back at the Snapdragon Inn. This place lights up when you're here—that's what Matilda always used to say, and she was right." Grandma Matilda's best friend hugged Zoey extra tight, and it felt good to see her again.

Gertrude, with big brown eyes and short, mousy brown hair, held onto one of the column posts, eyeing the slushy snow on the porch as she offered a thin-lipped smile. "I'm sorry we're barging in on you like this. Maybell wanted to beat Rosemary over here, but they're parking right now so—"

"We still beat them over here," Maybell told Gertrude with one arm still around Zoey.

"Them? Who's all coming?"

"Oh, I expect most the town will stop by sometime today to welcome you back to Woodstock," Gertrude said, extending a plate of cookies.

Maybell tucked her silver-blond hair behind her ear as she shook her head. "They want to know what you're doing with the inn. Rosemary said you weren't sure what you were doing with it, the liar."

*Oh, boy.*

"Maybell, I'm not sure what I'm going to do." The well of Zoey's guilt plunged deeper at the way Maybell's bright smile fell.

"Really? I know you were surprised at the reading, but I suppose I thought that after the idea of it sat with you for a little while, you'd realize how much this place means."

Gertrude braved crossing the porch to touch Maybell's arm to draw her attention. "She only just arrived, Maybell. Maybe this is too much for her."

"Pish posh, it's not too much for Zoey. You haven't seen this girl work as I have. She can run this place with her eyes closed once she gets it fixed into working order."

Gertrude gave Zoey a sympathetic look as Mrs.

Billings from the store—who Zoey then recalled was Rosemary Billings— climbed the stairs with a vanload of women following behind.

"Did I hear you say you're going to start fixing up the place? That's really for the best. It just can't be run the way it is. After the gazebo collapsed last year and Willard Shaw—he's a roofer, you remember him, don't you, dear? Well, he said the roof is only going to hold out another year, and that was last year."

"The whole roof?" Zoey asked.

"Not the *whole* roof," Maybell said, waving at Rosemary to try and shut her up.

Zoey felt the weight of the repairs begin to overwhelm her in a way she didn't feel she could handle. Grandma Matilda always got things fixed or knew who to call if she didn't know how to fix it herself. In New York, Zoey hounded the landlord of her apartment until he got a repairman out to fix any issues she had.

"Wow, it looks like there's a party going on down here," Jake said, coming up behind her.

Zoey stepped to the side so he could be included in the conversation. She was trying to figure out what it would take to get someone out to look at the roof in winter. Would the roof hold through the storm? What else was wrong with the house that she wasn't aware of?

"Well, we didn't mean to interrupt," Rosemary said with a blush and a grin in Jake's direction.

Zoey glanced Jake's way for the first time since he'd joined them and noticed his water-soaked white t-shirt.

"Ugh, the pipe on the sink gave me a hard time. It was leaking. I got it fixed, though."

"Mmmm, how nice," Rosemary said, sounding as though she didn't believe him.

Zoey wasn't as quiet as she once was as a little girl. Living in the city meant learning how to take care of yourself, and she'd learned in the past ten years how to do that for herself and others. "Yes, it was very nice of him to try and help me with the plumbing repairs. Your tone sounds like you think he was up to something else. What exactly?"

"Oh, no, I wasn't implying anything. Just surprised that your friend is wet and indoors since he told me how he was planning to shoot pictures today."

"Are you stopping by to welcome Zoey back into town?" Jake asked, cutting in before Zoey could come back at Rosemary.

Gertrude nodded. "I brought cookies. I hope you don't mind, but I'm not staying for the walkthrough. I want to beat the bad weather coming and get on home."

*Walkthrough?*

"Of course, no problem, Gertrude," Zoey said. "I wasn't prepared for a walkthrough. There's a bit of a mess."

"I'll do it with you so I can tell you about what needs polishing up. No need for all of us to go stomping through the house," Maybell volunteered quickly.

Zoey nodded thankfully. "I appreciate that. Thanks for coming by," she said to the others.

The women with Rosemary handed her and Jake pies, casseroles, sparkling cider, brownies, and all sorts of goodies. Most were friendly and well-meaning, but a few, like Rosemary, pushed to get answers about what would become of the Snapdragon Inn.

Maybell, although kind, wasn't subtle about how much she wanted Zoey to keep the inn as she walked her from room to room and over the backyard, noting all that was damaged. The fix-it list was long, and even if Jake knew how to do it all, they were going to need some help.

# CHAPTER 6

"I'll admit it's a lot to do, but at least you know your Grandma Matilda got estimates for all the work," Jake said after Maybell left. He'd traded his wet, white shirt for a navy-blue polo during the tour Maybell gave Zoey, but he was there for most of the tour.

Zoey nodded as she started up the stairs.

"You okay? Where are you going?" Jake asked, following her.

"I thought that I might find my Grandma Matilda's paperwork in her room. If I can find those estimates, it'll give me an idea of how much money I need to come up with."

Jake smiled. "Good thinking, and it'll also tell you what problems she was having with the house. Maybe we can fix some of them, so it won't be as much money as paying a professional."

"That's nice of you. Thanks, Jake."

Grandma Matilda's room was not a themed room unless that theme was artistically minded. Her grandmother wasn't a messy person when it came to most things—but paperwork, memorabilia, books, and drawings were an entirely different story.

"Finding the estimates could prove trickier than I thought," Zoey said, looking at the many stacks of papers and books.

"I'll help you comb through some of this for a little bit, and then I'll go get those pictures."

"You should probably go get your pictures. This could take a while."

Jake laughed. "Bet this is just organized chaos. As soon as you find one of the estimates, you'll have them all."

"I hope so," Zoey said.

They began to sort through the stacks, Zoey taking those closest to the bed and Jake taking on the pile of books. She found pictures and cards she'd made for her grandma when she was younger, and she found some that came from her mother when she was a girl. The thought of how little her mother had to do with Grandma Matilda, unless she wanted money, turned her stomach, and she quickly added the drawings to the box.

Afraid the whole stack was going to be filled with reminders of Zoey's absent mother, she went to put the entire stack in the box, but a few envelopes spilled out. She admitted that she would have to look through all of them in case one of the estimates got stuck in between the pages of memorabilia.

Jake returned from taking a stack of books to the library as Zoey picked up the envelopes. In her head, she was already trying to guess at numbers and attempting to do the math. Zoey would have missed what she held if Jake hadn't spoken up.

"These letters are nearly fifty years old. Look at the date on the stamp."

"You're right. They're from Joseph Harvey, my grandpa. I've never seen these before. My Grandma Matilda only spoke of him briefly from time to time. I think she missed him too much to speak of him more than she did." Zoey fanned out the stack of letters, surprised by how many there were, and to see that they were not all to Grandma Matilda. Some were to Grandpa Joseph from Grandma, too.

Jake made a profound sound that Zoey felt but couldn't express. "I bet you'll get to know him really well when you read the letters. Please tell me you're planning to read them. The journalist in me needs to know you are going to investigate."

Zoey laughed in agreement. "I definitely will read them." She found the white ribbon that must have come loose and tied the letters together, setting them aside to go back to read them when she got the chance.

As she continued through her stack, she proceeded at a slower pace to pay better attention to what she was looking at. Along with the letters, Zoey found old photo albums and journals, which she added to the stack of letters. The curiosity of what she might discover drew her attention back to the stack of letters, pictures, and journals repeatedly.

If her curiosity was piqued, Jake's must have been as hungry as a shark. Zoey had always seen Jake with a relaxed, easy-going demeanor, but seeing him at the edge of his seat like he was as he stared at the stack with wide, curious eyes, she couldn't help but laugh. Jake didn't even ask why she was laughing— he must have known how eager he appeared.

"How can you wait? I couldn't wait if I were in your shoes. I'm not even in your shoes, and I'm dying to know what you'll find out about your grandfather."

"I do want to dig into them, but we need to find those estimates."

Jake nodded. "Right, so I'll keep looking, and you start reading."

"Really? That doesn't make me feel like I'm helping if you're doing all the work."

"You're helping," he assured her. "Just dive in, and if you happen to read them aloud, that's totally fine." He winked at Zoey when she cocked her right brow at him. "I know, I'm shameless."

Picking up the letters and diaries, Zoey settled herself up on Grandma Matilda's bed. Maybe it was the storyteller in her, but she wanted to read them in the correct timeline order.

The journal belonging to Grandma Matilda had the earliest start date, so Zoey began with the journal. She also opened the photo albums and was happy to see they were in chronological order, at least as far as she could tell by the way Grandma Matilda continued to mature in the pictures.

There were a few pictures of Grandma Matilda as a baby, and more of her as a young girl, but it was quite early in the album that Grandma Matilda stopped being in the pictures and was most likely the one taking the photos.

A picture of a young man with the caption *A guy named Joe* written in Grandma Matilda's artistic handwriting was the earliest picture Zoey ever saw of her grandpa, and she stared at it, pouring over his youthful features and facial structure.

"Your eyes are shaped like his," Jake observed, looking at the picture over her shoulder.

"Yeah, they are. I never realized that before."

Zoey opened the journal, figuring that with all the free help Jake was offering, the least she could do was satisfy some of his curiosity.

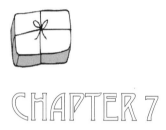

# CHAPTER 7

**Matilda Dunn's Diary**
**June 18, 1966**

I should have known better than to go to the abandoned Victorian house set on its own off the road and surrounded by overgrown vegetation to get some time to myself. Maybe I went there because I didn't actually want time to myself and secretly wanted Joseph Harvey to find me.

Of course, I did think it would take him longer to reach the forgotten Victorian from the heart of town. I didn't want him to see me crying. Joseph worries so much about making the people he cares for happy, and I knew I couldn't be another person in his life, making him sacrifice his happiness for mine.

He arrived not long after I did, and he was breathing faster so I knew he'd run the whole way and uphill at that. He asked me what was wrong, seeming to forget he was tired and crossed the living room area to take me in his arms.

I told him I was fine, but he could tell that wasn't true.

I finally told him his parents and my mom got together and had a talk. They want us to break up and give college a try with nothing holding us back.

I remember the exact words he said. "Yeah,

I know. They don't think we should try a long-distance relationship. It's not their decision, though, Matilda. It's ours."

Joseph looked so sure of himself, not at all the way his blue eyes faded when he talked about going to Stanford University. He was going to attend to please his family and carry on the tradition of the men in his family, who all went to Stanford. I didn't want to be away from Joseph, but I also didn't want him to miss out on a chance at an excellent education.

He told me he'd miss me terribly, and that I'm not just the woman he wants to goof around with. He said I'm his best friend and he doesn't feel like himself when I'm not around.

Joseph kissed me many times before, but this kiss was different. The way he kissed me started so eager and forceful but quickly softened, making that familiar flutter in my chest that happens when Joseph kisses me grow bigger than ever.

When our lips parted, and I looked up at him in the dim light of the Victorian, he ran his finger along my chin and said, "Matilda, you are my happiness." His declaration made my heart swell enough I thought it might burst and not because what he said was so lovely. It's because my Joseph is a man of few words. Which I've come to know means that he means every word that he speaks.

I should have told him that he is my happiness, too, but I kissed him again instead. Although we didn't kiss for long, we were both so happy we couldn't stop smiling and ended up laughing together. No one laughs like Joseph. His voice is so deep and somehow thrilling.

Next time his parents or my mom decide to tell me that Joseph and I are too young to know what we want, I'm going to think about how Joseph and I stayed out past curfew talking about how we could fix the abandoned Victorian and restore it to what it once was. I've always wanted to, and Joseph has always thought the soil was rich enough to grow most anything.

I don't know what will happen when Joseph goes away to college. It'll be the first time in almost six years that I'll be without him. He's been there for me when I've needed him. He was there when we lost Dad so suddenly in the fishing accident.

I still miss my dad. One thing losing him taught me, though, is that I was lucky to have him in my life and as my dad at all. So, I've decided that it's the same with Joseph. I'm fortunate to have had him in my life, and while I do, I'll love him so that when he's gone, he'll never doubt that he and I shared something special.

One thing is for sure. I refuse to be a moping, weeping willow like Jennifer Billings was after her boyfriend left for college last year. She's been such an Eeyore ever since. I refuse to be like that.

Tomorrow I think I'll take Jennifer with me to ride the Stuarts' horses. No one can be sad when there's that much wind in their hair. Too bad Joseph doesn't care for the smell of horses, though it's so cute the way his nose wrinkles even when he's just talking about the scent.

Thank you, Joseph, for being my first love. I hope you're my last love, too.

**July 4, 1966**

Joseph was selected by the mayor to be the one to read The Declaration of Independence at the July 4th celebration. Hearing our country's declaration of independence in Joseph's voice made my skin tingle, it was so moving. Everyone thought so, and Joseph didn't even want to stay and enjoy the compliments he was getting from the upper crust of Woodstock.

Joseph took my hand and said, "I've planned something for us, and your mom gave her permission as long as we bring another couple with us."

"Where are we going? What did you plan for us?" I was so excited even though I didn't have a clue as to what he'd planned. Maybell and Lincoln were in on the plan but wouldn't tell me where we were going when we climbed into Joseph's father's mint-green Falcon Sprint hardtop.

Joseph said very little and was smiling at me nearly the entire hour and a half drive. I was excited to have time with him. I never imagined he would've arranged for us to go to the famous Joe's Pond where there was a firework display.

They were all out of boats by the time we got there, but that didn't matter to me. Joseph brought a blanket for us in case we got cold, and we used it to spread out over the grass next to the pond.

Joseph let me lean against his chest and held me the entire time. I've never seen anything like the fireworks that were part of the show. They were magical like giant sparklers lit for just an instant across the sky.

On the ride home, Joseph reminded me that last year he and I read about the firework display in the paper. I don't remember it, but he did, and that's just like Joseph. He's so good at remembering things like that, and I'm happy he did.

# CHAPTER 8

Jake found the estimates in a folder buried under a pile of receipts. It was a staggering list, but Zoey was confident she could get the significant things fixed with what remained of the money that Grandma Matilda left her.

First thing on the list was to get the landline repaired. Cell phone signals were spotty in Woodstock and even more so with the dense forest surrounding the Snapdragon Inn. It was necessary to get the landline fixed so she could schedule the contractors essential for the work that Zoey wasn't skilled enough to do on her own.

Jake needed to leave to get the weather pictures he wanted but kept putting off his departure to help Zoey with the house. He only agreed to go and take the pictures once she assured him that she was going to be talking with the phone company and that was a one-person job.

The phone company reported that the line was already set up, but with the storm, a telephone pole came down. They assured her it was being fixed. That was the first bit of good news Zoey had about the repairs on the inn since she arrived.

When she left the building, the snow was starting to fall again in soft tufts, and since the wind died down, it wasn't too bad being outdoors in the snow. Zoey took a few pictures with her phone of the cloud formation and some footage of the town Christmas tree with the snow icing the tips of the beautiful evergreen.

"It's a beautiful tree," said a man standing not too far away from Zoey, and it startled her since she thought she was alone. "Sorry, didn't mean to scare you, Zoey." The man tipped back the brim of his snow hat.

"Mr. Bradshaw, I should have known it was you. That's your favorite hat, isn't it?"

He smiled softly. "I noticed the welcoming

committee stopped by the inn earlier. They're well-meaning but a touch overbearing."

"They are," Zoey agreed with a sigh. "Nice, but pushy."

"I imagine you got a lot of advice about how to run the Snapdragon Inn. My advice is to do it your way."

Zoey smiled and nodded. She didn't want to start the question and answer session that would go with telling him that she wasn't sure she would keep the inn.

"I know you've got your hands full sorting through things, but I hope you carved out some time to attend the Wassail Weekend?"

"I think I blocked out the festival in my head. I can't believe I forgot about it. Thanks for reminding me."

Mr. Bradshaw nodded, his smile growing. "You must be very sidetracked. There are flyers everywhere, and it's all anyone talks about. I imagine, though, with you, they want to know about the Snapdragon Inn. It would be good for you to take a break and have a little fun."

Zoey nodded though she wasn't sure she'd be able to have much fun with so much riding on the next few decisions she would make. "I'll try to be there."

"Bring your Mr. Jake along. I want to meet him."
He smiled, giving a little nod and walked away before
Zoey could let him know that Jake was not hers at all.
She returned to the Range Rover as she mentally kicked
herself. Usually, she was so much faster on the uptake.
Mr. Bradshaw was right—she was incredibly distracted.

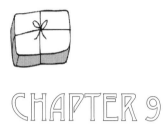

# CHAPTER 9

**Matilda Dunn's Diary**
**July 22, 1966**

Joseph doesn't want to be a lawyer. He has confided in me many times that he doesn't want to follow in the family footsteps and become an attorney. I know he is going to Stanford out of duty to his family. I should not have asked him to tell his parents how he feels. I was trying to help, and sure I don't want him to be so far away, but mostly, I want him to be happy. We fought about it, and I am scared. Soon, he'll be gone. I shouldn't have called him a coward. He said the way I do whatever I want to do is a disregard of the feelings of others. He thinks I'm selfish, and maybe he's right, but it hurts me so much that Joseph believes I am.

**July 30, 1966**

We aren't fighting anymore, but I'm still feeling afraid. I met Joseph at the Victorian for the last time. Joseph was there when I arrived. His golden-brown hair was newly cut in the same style as the one his father wears.

He told me he didn't have much time. His grandparents were waiting on him because they wanted to see him before he left for Stanford.

I tried my hardest to smile. I told him he looked handsome in his new suit and that I was very excited for him.

He seemed shocked and asked if I was telling the truth about being excited.

"Yes. You've earned your way to go, and it's a very prestigious school. I hope you're happy. That's all I want for you." I told him.

Joseph took my hands in his, and though his hands are usually warm, they were cold to the touch. He seemed worried by the way I was talking... like I was saying goodbye or something.

Joseph told me he would write to me often and that we'd be together forever.

I wanted to believe him, but he was trying so hard to please his parents, and I already knew how they felt about me. Only, I didn't want to fight with him, and I didn't want to make him sad when he should be excited to go to school.

I told him I would love getting letters from him. I kissed his cheek, and he turned his face so that my kiss landed square on his lips. My hands were shaking when I held onto his collar. I knew I was going to break down, so I pulled back.

He promised again that he would write, and he left.

Jenny Billings said that her boyfriend promised to write as well. Last week, Jenny heard that her boyfriend was engaged to be married in the fall. He'll be living in New York with his new bride. Soon he'll be probably enamored by the lights and events of the city as well as the new people.

As I watched Joseph turn away from me and leave the Victorian where we've talked about our dreams and confided in each other our grandest wishes, I couldn't help but feel like it would be the last time I would see him. I knew he wasn't the same as Jenny's boyfriend, but I never believed he was going to give in to the pressure of his family and take a path that he didn't want for his life. Yet, I was watching him walk that very path as he left.

I cried for a long while at the Victorian and even now that I'm home, I'm still shedding tears that won't stop. What if Joseph goes away and forgets all about me? What if he forgets about Woodstock or doesn't want to come back?

I think Jenny's entitled to a little more time as Eeyore, and maybe I deserve some time playing that role as well.

# CHAPTER 10

"Come in," Zoey called as she held the ladder steady for Herman Shroud, the electrician who was fixing the wiring on the gorgeous chandelier at the entranceway.

"I'll get it," Jake said, entering the foyer from the sitting room where he was shampooing the rug. He opened the front door and barely managed to get out of the way when Rosemary Billings and her entourage came barreling inside. "Come on in," Jake said, laughing off their pushy behavior.

Rosemary seemed to remember herself then and looked back at Jake. "Thank you very much, Mr. Ward. I apologize for rushing in this way but as you may have heard, the Wassail Weekend begins tomorrow, and Matilda drives one of the sleighs every year." Rosemary looked directly at Zoey as she said the last part.

"I don't know how to drive a sleigh, Mrs. Billings," Zoey said, shaking her head.

"That's all right, dear," Mrs. Billings said a bit too sweetly for Zoey to feel at ease. "Maybell said that if you weren't comfortable driving Santa's sleigh in the parade, you could take her place leading one of the ponies."

Zoey noticed Jake's hand covering up the massive smile on his face as he listened Mrs. Billings cornering her into participating.

"This way, you'll be ready to go to the Memory Tree lighting straight after the parade." Mrs. Billings turned around to address Jake. "The Memory Tree lighting ceremony is done in memory of all who have passed. There are bonfires and plenty of hot drinks and goodies to enjoy, too. You'll be there taking pictures, of course."

Jake nodded. "I wouldn't miss it."

"Great, then it's all settled. Be sure to arrive at one o'clock to get your Christmas costume and be assigned your pony," Mrs. Billings said to Zoey with a triumphant smile. "Matilda would surely be delighted to see you participating in the festivities."

Herman began climbing down the ladder, and Zoey held it firmly as she smiled at the chandelier that was once again working and shining in all its glory.

"I don't know if you heard, Zoey, but my sister Jenny passed this year as well. So, I will be grieving, too, if you need someone to stand with," Mrs. Billings offered, both surprising Zoey with her kindness and reminding her of the mention of Jenny Billings in Grandma Matilda's diary.

"Thank you. I'm sorry for your loss, Mrs. Billings."

Mrs. Billings nodded as she put her white-gloved hand on her chest. "It is hard to deal with loss. All we can do is carry on their memory—as it looks like you are doing with the Snapdragon Inn. It's a relief to know you're staying on and honoring Matilda after all."

*So much for Mrs. Billings being less pushy.*

"I'm making sure that the inn is properly repaired. I haven't made my decision about what I'll do with it once I've finished."

Mrs. Billings frowned, letting out a long-suffering sigh. "Well, the Snapdragon Inn is a jewel to this town.

You could always leave it to the town so that it can be kept up in the way Matilda would have wanted it. Selling to some stranger lends no guarantee that this magnificent Victorian structure will be respected and upheld. You wouldn't want some outsider to come in and tear down walls or ruin the gardens. That would leave Matilda in a state of unrest to suffer so much to happen to her legacy."

Swallowing the lump of what was probably guilt, Zoey nodded. "I hadn't thought of leaving it to the city. I'll have to consider that."

"I hope you do, as it's really the only option," one of Rosemary Billings cohorts agreed.

"Well," Zoey said, ready for Mrs. Billings and her staring entourage to get going, "the festivities begin today, don't they? You should be going. I don't want you to miss them."

"I've already walked to the Artisan Market. The history center doesn't open for the Wassail Open House until five, so we have plenty of time. Don't you worry. Come along, ladies, we should be going so these two can get dressed and join in on all the festivities they're missing." Mrs. Billings said.

Jake opened the door for them, and each lady

smiled at him on their way out. Mrs. Billings stopped at the door and put her hand on his arm. "I wanted to give you permission to take my picture at the Memory Tree tomorrow. I know you'll want to commemorate the event with someone whose roots are deep in this town."

"Thank you," Jake said, doing an excellent job of keeping a straight face. "See you at the Open House." Jake waved and shut the door before Mrs. Billings could volunteer to be photographed there as well.

"I think Jenny must have been the quieter sister," Jake chuckled.

Herman nodded. "She was. Nicer, too." He clapped his hands together and then peeled off his gloves. "You're all set now. Even got the wiring fixed for you all the way around on the wraparound porch."

"Thank you, Herman." Zoey smiled. "I love seeing the chandelier all lit up like this."

"You bet. I'll drop your invoice in your mailbox. Happy Holidays." Herman collapsed the ladder and started for the door before pausing. "Would you like a word of advice?"

Zoey tried to smile, but the tension in her shoulders at such a monumental decision made it difficult. "Sure."

"Let the rope out when you lead the ponies. If you

stand too close, they sometimes bite." He fixed his winter hat onto his head. "As for the house? Keep it. It suits you both quite well."

Herman steered the ladder through the open doorway, nearly taking out the window next to the door, so Zoey didn't dare distract him further by correcting him about Jake.

"Thanks again," Jake said and closed the door behind Herman. Jake went to Zoey and surprised her with a hug. "Everyone is going to have their opinion, but I know your grandma would want you to be happy more than anything else. Do what's right for you."

Zoey leaned into him, hugging him back. She had not realized just how much she needed that hug and show of support. The green flannel shirt he wore smelled like a combination of sandalwood and the carpet shampoo. It made her smile. "This all would have been so much for me to take on. I mean, it is, but with you here, I've been able to keep going and keep my head clear enough to function. Thank you, Jake. You're a wonderful friend."

# CHAPTER 11

**September 2, 1966**

Dear Matilda,

It's been ten long days since I saw you last. There was so much that I wanted to say to you. Having to go was so hard already, and I knew that if I told you just how much I love you, I would not have had the strength to go. I had to go.

I know that you said that money isn't important to you, but I want to buy you the

Victorian so you can do all the things you talked about doing. Hopefully, you know that I'm telling you the truth.

Stanford has a big campus, and it's a beautiful enough school, but it'll never compare to any place that has you. I miss you, Matilda. Do you miss me? I hope you're not angry or disappointed in me for going.

Please write me back. I've never missed anyone or anything so much as I miss you.


Forever yours,

Joseph

**September 10, 1966**


Dear Matilda,

I haven't heard from you, and I'm hoping it

is because the mail is slow and not because you have already forgotten me. Or worse, because you hate me.

The friends I've made here remind me of my father and my brothers. They are nice enough, but I'm nothing like them. It's hard to stay here and be true to my word that I would attend Stanford when it feels like I'm a piece of a puzzle that just doesn't fit here.

Mom wrote me a letter that mentioned you. She said that she saw you with a group of friends at the café. At least I know you are well. I want you to be happy even if I am miserable without you. If you're happy, I hope it's because you know wherever you are, you have my heart.

I am missing you.

Forever yours,
Joseph

**September 14, 1966**

Dear Matilda,

Please don't say I told you so, but I just finished the first test in my pre-law class with Professor Hildred. So many students in his class leave in tears because the material is challenging to remember and understand. My father has spoken of very little besides law, and so it was easy for me. That should have made me happy, but it didn't.

I know being an attorney has excellent potential for making money. But it's just not what I want. It's worth it if it means I can provide for us, but it's not worth it if it means I'll be losing you.

Sometimes I wish I was as brave as you are about saying what you want. I wish I could have made my father hear me when I told him I didn't want to go to Stanford. Trying to make him happy is looking like a long and lonely road.

I miss talking to you. You give great advice and even when you listen, it helps me. I guess that's why I wrote this letter— to speak to you and remind you that I need you. I hope you're saving a place for me in the puzzle of your life. I love you, Matilda.


Forever yours,

Joseph


P.S. Eddy Collison is my roommate here at college, and he's told me more than twice that he's done hearing about the beautiful Matilda Dunn in Woodstock, Vermont. I talk about you all the time. Tonight, there's a campus party, and Eddy insisted that I go with him. I wish you were going to be there.

### September 18, 1966

My dear Joseph,

I promised your mom that I would wait until September before I wrote you so that you would get a chance to adjust, but after reading your letters, I can't let you believe that I don't miss you terribly. I do. I miss you so much it hurts, and it's not getting better with time like my mom says it will.

Going to Stanford and trying was very brave. Leaving everything and everyone you know to try anything at all is brave, and I don't want you to think that you aren't courageous. My Joseph Harvey is brave, kind, and loyal. So, I won't have you saying anything else.

Also, don't tell your mom I told you about the promise. Okay?

If law school is easy, maybe you should stick with it. I don't think there are very many people who would say it's easy, but you always were extraordinarily bright.

Eddy better not drag you anywhere you don't want to go. Did you have fun at the party? Was it exciting? Did you want to dance with anyone? I want you to be happy, and so you don't have to tell me if you did dance with another girl. Just, please tell me if we're breaking up and don't make me hear that you're engaged from your family like Jenny's boyfriend. Okay?

Missing you,
Matilda

P.S. No matter what, there's always a place for you in my life puzzle, Joseph Harvey.

**September 21, 1966**

Dear Matilda,

Please don't make any more promises like
that with anyone in my family. It was awful not
to hear from you for so long. I'm sure my mother
meant well, but she and Dad don't understand
what you and I have together.

As for school being easy, I may have spoken
too soon. It's becoming more challenging and the
only part of my day that I look forward to is
checking the mail for letters from you. I hope
you're not going to make me wait for the next
letter to come in September. Please don't do that
to me.

I did go to the party, but I wasn't tempted
to dance with any of the girls there. Sure, there
were pretty girls, but none of them were you. You
are the only girl I want to dance with, even
though I don't dance well enough to impress a

toddler—I'm still saving every terrible move for you.

Dad wrote to me to tell me he spoke to Professor Hildred and was displeased about my not volunteering to be the head of the study group for the class. He also said before I even got my last exam back that I got a C. I don't have to tell you how much Dad prizes grades.

I'll be joining the study group, but I did write Dad back. I told him that I don't want to be in law school and that I only came to make him proud of me. His next letter will be a handful of pages all telling me how lucky I am to be at Stanford.

Is it so terrible not to live my life the way he wants me to?

I miss you more every day.


Forever yours,

Joseph

# CHAPTER 12

The carpet shampooer suctioned up the last section on the rug in the foyer. Zoey hit the off switch and wiped her wet brow with the back of her hand. Jake said he would finish the rugs when he returned from the festivities that evening, but after reading a handful of the letters between her Grandpa Joseph and Grandma Matilda, she felt restless.

Taking a step back, she took in the scene, wishing that she'd taken before pictures to compare with after pictures. The rugs that didn't have runs in them were worth trying to save, and that was why she'd rented the carpet cleaner. It paid off because the rug under the chandelier looked almost brand new.

It was beautiful, and she was proud of the work she'd done so far but was that enough of a reason to give up her career in New York?

Too restless to stand still, Zoey hefted one of the rugs that had too many snags to be saved out to the garbage. It was heavy and so dusty that Zoey did her best not to breathe. Nearly halfway to her destination, her cell phone started ringing in her pocket.

*Of course, I have a signal out here on the driveway.*

Zoey rushed to get to the garbage can. Two rings… three rings… four rings… five rings…. She dropped the carpet next to the closed garbage can and dug out her phone. "Hello?"

"Is this Zoey Larson?"

She recognized Celeste's voice from the office back in New York. "Hello, Celeste, yes, this is she."

"I'm surprised you're still alive. I've been calling and trying to reach you for the last thirty minutes."

*No answer in thirty minutes means I'm dead? Sheesh.*

"Sorry. There's spotty reception up here. Is there something I need to know?"

Celeste sucked in a breath. "Oh, my priceless

fountain pen, yes! I'm calling because Georgette Newari is pregnant and decided to be a stay-at-home mom. Can you believe that?"

"Uh, I suppose so. Why would I—"

"I think that fresh air is getting to you, babe. I'm calling on behalf of Kenzie Highsmith to offer you the promotion of becoming Senior Lead Journalist and take Georgette's place before she has the mom-brain fog clear from her head and calls wanting her job back."

*Senior Lead Journalist?*

"Hello? Did I lose you? Stupid mountains."

"No… no, I'm here."

*Do I take it? What about the Snapdragon Inn?*

"Do I answer now?" Zoey choked out, hating the weight of pressure pounding through her head.

Celeste sighed. "Well, technically, you can only accept after you speak with Ms. Highsmith, but I know you're no dummy. When you get back, all you'll have to do is sign on the dotted line, and the job will be yours. Merry Christmas, m'kay, doll? Bye."

"Celeste, I need to think about it…. Celeste?" Zoey looked at her phone screen to confirm what she already knew. Celeste had disconnected before Zoey could respond. Frustration, fatigue, and indecision made her want to scream. Instead, she threw open the lid on the garbage can, hefted the rolled-up rug, and smashed it into the can. It took a lot of hitting and shoving, even a jump or two from the top to get the rug to fit inside, but Zoey managed it.

Climbing out of the trash can without tipping it over was made possible with the help of a strong tree branch Zoey used to steady herself.

*Senior Lead Journalist? Me? That means they skipped over Sharon, Craig, and Megan— and picked me.*

The inn was toasty warm, smelling of roasted marshmallows and the apple pie one of the townspeople brought over that was warming in the oven. No place in the world felt more like home than the Snapdragon Inn.

"Grandpa Joseph, I think I know how you felt when you were at Stanford. I can't believe I have to make this choice at all. Grandma should be here."

*Stop complaining. Pick yourself up. Get to work.*

After she took out the apple pie, Zoey set it to cool and went to work polishing the newly exposed hardwood floor where the rug she just tossed used to lay.

"The sun is going down; you're losing light," Jake said, startling her from the job at hand. She hadn't realized how she'd let time get away from her while she moved from room to room polishing the floors where the rugs had to be removed. "Are you all right?"

Zoey nodded, but as she sat back on her feet, she shook her head. "I got a call from Celeste today, and I was offered a promotion to Senior Lead Journalist."

"That's... I mean, wow. That's incredible!" He started to take a step toward her and then stopped. "Wait, you said you're not okay. You don't want the promotion?"

"I do. But... I want this place, too. It's my childhood home, and it carries a piece of my grandparents and of me. There are so many memories, and so many ideas I have on how to fix it up."

Jake scratched at the dark stubble on his chin. "This place is going to take a lot of work to get it back on its feet."

Zoey nodded, seeing for herself that it was true.

"The position at Birdseye isn't going to wait around for you either, and it's a demanding job. You wouldn't have time to come here and check on your house."

"I realize that," Zoey said.

"Which one means more to you?"

It was hard not to vent her frustration at Jake. He

was asking the same questions she already asked herself. "I've killed myself trying to be taken seriously as a journalist at Birdseye."

"Then there ya go." Jake nodded.

"But I couldn't rest easy knowing I gave this house to some stranger. This is my home, and I felt that way even before Grandma Matilda left it to me."

Jake shook his head and shrugged. "We could talk in circles, but this is a choice you have to make yourself. The regrets I have are usually from not trying, and you're here trying. You've got a list of what you'll have to do to get this place going, and you know what it's like to live here. You have been killing it at Birdseye and in New York, so you know what that road will be like."

She knew he was trying to help, but he was telling her what she already knew, and it wasn't making her choice easier, or any clearer.

Zoey wiped her hands on the hand towel at her waist and stood. She couldn't sit in indecision forever. "I suppose I could give the Snapdragon Inn to the city."

"I warmed up the apple pie again. I'll make some hot chocolate, and maybe you'll feel better with a little something in your stomach. You should never make a big choice when you're hungry and tired."

"Thanks, Jake."

His smile grew, and his chuckle drew her attention. "What?"

"I want to help, I do— but I also really want to know what happens next with Matilda and Joseph. I don't know how you can put the letters and journal down mid-story like that. So, I guess I'm admitting that I hope we'll peruse the letters and all that while we take a break from work. What do ya say?"

Zoey shook her head, trying not to burst out laughing. He knew just as she did that Joseph was her grandfather, so it was safe to assume they worked it all out. Then again, reading about how Grandma Matilda and Grandpa Joseph had been meeting at 'the Victorian' long before they were even married made the inn feel like a lifeline that still connected her to them even though they had passed.

Having a tie to them as she made her choice about which way to go in this fork in the road of her life seemed like a good idea. "Yeah. Let's see how they figure out what they will do. Maybe it'll help me because I'm at a loss."

# CHAPTER 13

**Matilda Dunn's Diary**
**November 18, 1966**

Thanksgiving is coming, and Joseph will be coming home to Woodstock. It's what I've wanted for months but now that it's around the corner... I'm nervous.

I've been working hard saving up to buy the Victorian, and I have a long way to go, but that's okay because I know it's what I want. Still, all this working and being an adult stuff has me looking at things in my life differently than when I was still in school.

Joseph has been living independently from home, family, and me. Surely, that has changed him. I know my love for him hasn't changed. My feelings for him haven't dimmed at all, but I remember him as he was and what if he's different? What if he comes back so different that he's not the Joseph I love anymore?

What if he comes back and I love him still, but he sees me differently, too? What if I've changed too much and he can't see in me who he fell in love with?

I'm nervous.

He writes to me and tells me that he loves me, and he also tells me that he doesn't want to be at Stanford—but he's still there. I know he's trying to do right by his family, but it makes me nervous to see him say one thing and do another.

I don't know what he wants anymore, and I won't know until I see him and look into his eyes.

He says I'm brave. If I'm so courageous, why am I so afraid to see the man I love?

### *November 22, 1966*

I have been taking on extra shifts where I can get them between the market and the Café in town. It's easier to forget to worry when I'm too busy working or too exhausted to let my mind wander and discover new things to be worried about.

A guy named Wallace comes into the café often. He's from Hartland, which isn't too terribly far from Woodstock. He works in real estate, which could be very helpful in acquiring the Victorian.

Wallace is nice enough, but he's not Joseph.

He's asked me out a few times, but I told him that I had a boyfriend. Somehow, he found out that my boyfriend is away at school and so he's become a squeaky wheel in my ear, telling me about how my boyfriend is dating and having a great time in school with other girls. Wallace says things that stick with me, like, "You don't want to let your life pass you by while you're waiting around standing still, do you?"

I know he's got an agenda, but there has to be some truth in what he's saying if it's repeating in my mind. Maybe the best thing for Joseph and me is to break up. Perhaps he needs to be free to decide for himself what he wants. I don't want him to blame me if it turns out he would rather be somewhere else or be with someone else.

Joseph is who I want, and that hasn't changed, but I'm not going out and having fun like I would be if I were single. I don't want to regret this time in my life and see it as stagnant.

More than anything, I don't want to lose Joseph. How am I going to tell him this without losing him?

# CHAPTER 14

"I'm surprised you were able to get the lumber in so quickly during the holidays," Zoey said as she wrote out a check from her inheritance account.

"Herman is installing these for you? If he's booked up, I got a guy who can help you," Ernest of Woodstock Home and Hardware offered.

Zoey handed him the check. "Thank you. If you have the contact information for him, that would be great."

"Sure thing," Ernest said, pulling a notebook from his coat pocket. "Are you going to make your way to the Wassail Weekend? I heard you were leading ponies."

*I forgot how quickly word travels even with innocuous bits of information like leading ponies.*

"It's seven in the morning, and that isn't until later this afternoon, so I've got plenty of time. I'll be there. Are you participating in the parade this year?"

Ernest nodded but didn't volunteer in what capacity. Instead, he started asking questions. "The Snapdragon Inn sure is a big responsibility. It seems to me that the choice is simple, isn't it?"

"Is it?" Zoey sighed, glancing down at the half-written contact information on the notepad. She began to weigh how badly she wanted that information. Enough to stand there and be peppered with questions about the inn?

"Sure. Take a look at how the whole town comes together to celebrate the Wassail Weekend. Every person volunteers to do their special part. Most don't even have to be asked because they are already doing the asking—wanting to know what they can do."

*And that's a jab at me for having to be asked? He has got to be joking.*

"Imagine how quickly the Snapdragon Inn would be restored. Woodstock is a special place with exceptional, generous people who take care of each other and what's important. It's not like in the city where people would sell their relative for a month of free rent."

"Do you have a lot of experience with city life then, Ernest? I remember you working here back when I was in middle school, and that's been a lot of years."

Ernest ripped the page from the pad. "Don't need to waste more than an hour in hell to know it's hot, ma'am." He laughed. "I can see you're getting upset, but that's not worth doing. I'm just offering you some sound, friendly advice. The Snapdragon Inn already belongs to Woodstock— might as well make it official."

"Thank you for the lumber and the contact information," Zoey said, taking the paper from his hand.

"Enjoy the parade." Ernest smiled.

Zoey knew that if she were in New York dealing with a man like Ernest, she would have told him his unwanted advice was skewed to make her feel obligated to give away what Grandma left to her. But she wasn't in New York City. Woodstock was a small place, which meant one could not go around losing their temper and burning bridges. Indulging in that kind of behavior would only close doors in the community for Zoey, and it would have upset Grandma Matilda if she were still alive to hear about any such bad behavior.

The Range Rover fired up easily. She planned on stopping at Mac's Market to pick up more eggs, but she didn't want to run the risk of bumping into other stubborn members of the community. In the mood she was in, Zoey was liable to cut loose and let someone have it.

An icy patch on the road sent the Range Rover turning toward the oncoming lane of traffic. Zoey tapped the brake lightly and turned the wheel. Her heart hammered as she watched the horizon where a car could appear at the crest of the hill and barrel into her if she didn't get in control of her vehicle.

"Don't panic," she told herself, noting that the slide was slow. That meant it would be easier to stop. Zoey tapped the brakes again. "Come on," she rasped, knowing she had to stop holding her breath but was too tense to draw in air. The boards in the back shifted, changing the balance of weight. The slide sped up, but then the tires took hold of the road and Zoey was able to maneuver the vehicle.

The road was too narrow to pull off to the side. Breathing hard, she pressed forward. Hands shaking, Zoey reminded herself that she was all right. She took several deep breaths to reclaim her calm, then ignored her still quivering fingers on the steering wheel, concentrating on the road.

The hands-free phone option on the car scared her as the ringing blasted over the speakers. Zoey considered not answering but then what if it was someone from Birdseye calling? With white knuckles on the wheel, she let the phone ring several times before tapping the button on the steering wheel to answer.

"This is Zoey Larson. Can I help you?" Even her voice sounded shaky.

*Get a grip, Zoey.*

"Ms. Larson, how are you?" The familiar soothing, masculine voice of Grandma Matilda's attorney sounded over the speakers.

Zoey waited for Mr. Pearson to continue, and when he didn't, she realized he wanted her to answer. "Fine. I'm fine. How are you?"

"That's wonderful to hear. Someone mentioned to me the other day that you were looking a bit weighed down and unrested."

"Nope, I'm just fine," Zoey said, doing her best not to sound snappy or rude. It wasn't his fault that people in small towns often scrutinized each other and passed on their assumptions. "Do you get to take the weekend off so you can enjoy the Wassail celebrations?"

*Ten more minutes, and I'll be back at the inn. That's nothing. Just take it nice and slow.*

"Oh, I make sure to stop and enjoy the holidays even when I do have to put in a few hours at the office. Time goes by too fast to let work be the only thing I do." He laughed.

Zoey attempted a chuckle that came out weak and strained even to her own ears.

"The reason I'm calling you, Ms. Larson, is because I decided to swing by my office for a couple of hours this morning, and I thought that if you wanted to get the paperwork started for transferring the deed, I could begin drawing up some of the forms."

"I'm sorry, I guess I don't understand. I thought the transfer of the deed paperwork from Grandma to me was completed last month?"

There was a long pause following Zoey's question that made her think she might have lost signal, but then Mr. Pearson said, "I believe I must have misunderstood what I heard from Rosemary Billings. She seemed so sure of herself when I spoke with her a few minutes ago that I... Well, that goes to show that I've got to do a better job listening, I suppose."

"Misunderstood what?" Zoey asked, already forming a pretty good idea for herself but wanting to hear it from him.

"I'm sure I misunderstood, but I thought she told me that you were transferring the deed to the city. I should have waited for you to contact me, of course. It's just that I was already in the office and I'll be leaving before noon to join in the festivities."

*Deep breath in, slow breath out.*

"Mr. Pearson, I'm sure you didn't misunderstand Rosemary Billings. However, she does not speak for me or know what I am or am not doing with the inn. Neither does Ernest, Herman, Mr. Bradshaw, Maybell, or anyone else."

He coughed quietly on his end before he spoke again. "I can see now that I fell prey to town speculation again. I do hope you know that I am happy to execute any order or contract you may need regarding the property, but of course, I wish you nothing but the best if you elect to remain in ownership of the Snapdragon."

"Thank you."

Zoey noticed as she turned into the driveway of the inn that her hands were beginning to ache because of how tightly she gripped the steering wheel.

"I'll see you at the parade then. Have a Merry Christmas, Ms. Larson."

"Merry Christmas," Zoey said and tapped the end button on the steering wheel with her thumb. *I am going to knock Rosemary off her high horse and kick her out of my house the next time she dares show her fake smile on my property again. I ought to drive back to town right now and find that meddling old bitty. How dare she speak to anyone on my behalf!* Shifting the Range Rover into park, Zoey unbuckled her seat belt.

Not in the mood to wait for the garage door to open and close, Zoey parked in front of the garage door next to Jake's car. Sliding off the seat, she gasped as the deep snow climbed up the inside of the jeans she borrowed from her grandma's things. The snow reached the inside of the bend of her knee and would have won a shriek from her had she not been clenching her teeth.

"So cold," Zoey growled as she lifted her legs one by one and shook the snow from her pant legs. "I'll take a hot shower. I'm fine. I handled the situation with the lawyer, and he knows I'm not just giving away Grandma's Victorian. I'm not giving up my choices and letting others decide what I'll do with my life for me. I've got this."

114

Zoey exhaled slowly feeling eyes on her as she did.

"Good morning, Zoey," Mr. Bradshaw said when she looked in the direction of his house off to the left. Mr. Bradshaw stood at the property line, close enough to have heard the pep talk she gave herself. "I got to baking last night, and I thought you and your guest might like some muffins."

He wasn't holding anything and must have read the confusion on Zoey's face because he added, "I dropped them off to your houseguest just now."

"Thank you." Zoey could feel the burn in her blushing cheeks. It was a wonder how any more blood could fill her head than was already there after the morning she'd had.

"Merry Christmas," Mr. Bradshaw said as he smiled to himself and continued his trek back to his house.

*This feels nothing like Christmas. This feels more like the world having a laugh at my expense.*

Zoey shoved the door shut on the Rover. Each step she took back toward the house was a test of endurance as the snow-packed into her pants around her ankles, shins, and calves. It wasn't a long walk to the front porch where she'd cleared the snow earlier that same morning, but the skin on her legs was numb and wet as she

115

knocked the snow from her pants.

The front door was unlocked.

*You can't leave a front door unlocked, Jake. This isn't New York City but still.*

After all the trouble she went through to get the rugs and floors cleaned, she didn't want to make tracks through the house. Zoey took off her socks and shoes. She entered and was about to close the front door when she heard the rustling of papers coming from the dining room.

Making quick work of closing the front door and rolling up her wet pants, Zoey followed the noise.

Jake sat at the dining room table with the letters, diaries, and photo albums spread out around him as he proceeded to open another letter and begin reading it as she watched frozen in place from the doorway. Gulping air, Zoey tried to make sense of what she saw. No matter how she tried, she couldn't come up with a reasonable explanation for what she was witnessing.

"Jake? What are you doing?"

He lowered the letter in his hand and looked over his shoulder at her, his green eyes widening as he took her in. "Zoey, you look upset. It's not what it seems."

"No? So, you're not going through my family's

personal documents? It sure looks like that's what you're doing." Zoey pulled the letter out of his hand as she eyed the screen on his laptop.

"I'm not going through them to give in to my curiosity. I'm going to write a feature about the Snapdragon, about your grandparents. This is such a rich history—"

"My history," Zoey snapped, cutting him off. "These letters and journals were written by my family. They belong to me. What made you think you had the right to go through them without my permission, much less share them with the world?"

Jake stood and started returning the letters to their envelopes.

"No, don't touch them. You do not have permission to comb through my grandparents' things like this. I should never have shared any of it with you. I thought you'd be civilized enough to recognize the difference between my own family history and some article."

"I was trying to honor your grandparents, what they built together and their lives, but you're right, I should have asked. That said, you did choose to share the letters with me. You invited me to read them with you, which I thought meant that you didn't mind sharing with me or anyone else what amazing people your Grandma Matilda and Grandpa Joseph were."

Zoey closed his laptop and handed it to him. "You aren't just anybody, Jake. I thought we were friends. Clearly, I was reading too much into things. From now on, I'll be sure to let you know what's on and off the record."

Jake accepted the laptop, and his green eyes were solemn as they looked into Zoey's, but he said nothing more. She watched as he picked up his coat off the coatrack. "I apologize for overstepping." His words were stilted, and though he kept his facial expressions stoic, Zoey saw in his eyes that she'd hurt him.

Without responding, she watched him walk out the front door with his laptop under one arm and his coat draped over his left shoulder. His beanie was still on the hook, but he left it there or didn't see it. The door closed between them, and Zoey turned back to the stack of letters.

Some of the letters he'd opened were ones she had not read yet. Gritting her teeth, she moved them back into the box she'd stored them in earlier and took them with her upstairs to her bedroom. It was only mid-morning, and she was already emotionally exhausted and wanted to go back to bed and hide for the remainder of the day.

Grandma Matilda would never have allowed her to wallow over a stressful morning. When she was younger, it wasn't always easy to appreciate having Grandma Matilda there to push her and remind her how important it was to get back up.

More than anything else, Zoey wanted to ask Grandma Matilda what to do. Not just to get her input on what choice she should make, but also how to deal with the people of Woodstock and their pushiness. How could she get them to back off and give her room to figure out what she wanted to do without being rude and offending people who were near and dear to Grandma Matilda?

How was she going to deal with Jake?

An hour had passed since he left, which gave her some cooling down time. While warming her feet in the shower, she replayed all that she'd said to him.

Zoey knew that she had a right to say most of what she did, but the way she raised her voice and the vehemence behind her accusatory statements wasn't meant for him. The aggravating morning she'd spent being harassed about the Snapdragon Inn had charged her up, so when he'd overstepped, she ran him over like

119

a deer frozen in her headlights.

He'd said a few choice statements, too, trying to make her feel responsible for his invasion because she trusted him enough to share with him. It was enough to keep her temper simmering even though she was the one to come charging at him and put him on the defensive.

One thing was for sure. Instead of coming across clear and without malice—as Grandma Matilda did, making it appear effortless—Zoey had taken a situation that was already proving difficult and made it worse.

*This is why living in a big city is easier. If you mess things up with one person, there is always another person to befriend.*

Zoey's gaze was drawn to the closet where she put the box. She could practically hear Grandma Matilda gasping at her thoughts. No doubt she would ask her why she took such a lazy approach to the relationships in her life or something to that effect that would be a true statement about choosing shallow and meaningless over deep, quality connections.

"Nothing is ever easy, is it, Grandma Matilda?"

# CHAPTER 15

**Matilda Dunn's Diary**
**November 25, 1966**

When I went to meet Joseph at the Victorian, I was sure that when I saw him it was going to be so much harder to tell him that he and I should take a step back. My heart was hammering so hard, and I was so scared that I considered writing a letter and just handing it to him.

I arrived first, and so I got to see him

before he saw me. Joseph had continued to mature and grow. He looked taller, and his clothes were neat as a pin—just like when I'd first met him before I convinced him to relax a little. I noticed that he looked thinner, and his eyes had a sad, almost tormented look about them. He walked with his shoulders slumped even though his steps were sure and fast. I could see that my Joseph was torn and hurting.

That made telling him what I did easier because I knew it would be better for him. Joseph was happy to see me, and it did break my heart to have to tell him we needed to step back and just be friends while he was away at school.

It was the hardest thing I've ever had to do.

Now that it's done, I feel sad, lonesome, and needy for Joseph's reassurance that we will remain friends. I don't understand how doing the right thing can hurt so much.

**December 1, 1966**

Dear Joseph,

I went to your house to see you before you returned to school, but you'd already left. Your mom still isn't a big fan of mine, in case you were wondering. This time, I can't blame her, if what I said to you at the Victorian hurt you.

Hurting you is the last thing in the world I wanted to do. I hoped that I was clear when I told you that my feelings for you haven't changed. I meant it when I said that. I love you, Joseph Harvey, and I know I always will. All that I want is for you to be free to make your own choice. I've seen you struggling with what to do, and I believe that by taking a step back, you can make your choices for yourself.

I would never want you to wonder what decisions you might have made if you hadn't been worrying about how I would feel about them.

123

Make your choices knowing that no matter what, we'll always be friends.

With love,

Matilda

**December 5, 1966**

Dear Matilda,

I'm thrilled that you wrote to me.

When we spoke at the Victorian, I was distraught, and I don't think I heard much of what you said after you explained that you felt we should take a step back. I've been a mess, feeling like I've lost the only woman who truly knows me, my friend, and the woman I've dreamed of making my wife.

I don't agree with you that we should take

a step back. There are few things in this world that I am sure of and the two of us is one of them. However, I see why you think we need to. You're not wrong that I need to decide what to do with my life, but I need more time.

It's not enough that I know I don't want to be a litigator. I need to figure out what I am going to do and how I'm going to earn a living so that when I speak with my parents again, they will take me seriously.

As for my mom, I don't think she understood how much you mean to me until she saw me after I thought I'd lost you.

I don't want to take a step back. I'm glad we'll still be friends, but I want more than that. Please don't push me away.


Forever yours,

Joseph

**December 18, 1966**

Dear Matilda,

Your continued insistence that we take a step back at least until I've made a decision is frustrating and feels like a punishment even if that isn't your intention.

I've been working hard and doing a lot of thinking. Examining my likes and dislikes, focusing on what I'm good at. I'm sure that very soon I'm going to know what it is I want to pursue. Since I know that what I want isn't going to be found here at Stanford, I'm thinking of leaving.

You know that if I were to do this, it's very likely that my father won't be speaking to me. I don't want to dishonor him or act ungrateful for his mentoring and for helping me to get into Stanford. Honestly, I think disappointing and hurting him has always been the force at my back pushing me to Stanford and in following in his footsteps.

I still don't know what I'm going to do or how I'm going to stop attending Stanford without ruining the bond between my father and me. He breathes Stanford he loves it so much.

Maybe you'll read this letter and see that I'm taking steps and thinking about my choices. Perhaps you'll see that taking a step back was a good idea and now it's time to take a step forward?

As for me, in my heart, I haven't stepped back, and I don't think I ever could. I love you. I always will.

Forever yours,

Joseph

P.S. I'll be home for Christmas break and step back or not, I can't wait to kiss you when I see you.

# CHAPTER 16

Zoey pulled the string attached to the light and gave a grateful sigh as the attic lit up. It was a lovely surprise to find that while Grandma Matilda's bedroom was organized chaos, the attic was neatly organized.

While Zoey was reading more of her grandparents' history, she was also dreading the Wassail Weekend later that day. It was while she was reading that she suddenly remembered Grandma Matilda's Wassail costume. If she arrived at the parade in Grandma Matilda's costume, it would be a show of support to the town, and it would also show to them that she did honor Grandma Matilda. It might not be enough to stop them from trying to influence her decisions, but at least it would be a peaceful way of making her point.

The first stack of boxes Zoey found was labeled Easter and spring décor. The second was labeled Halloween, the fourth autumn. When she saw the stack covering one whole wall, she knew she'd found the right one even before she found the label she was searching for— Christmas décor.

"Okay, where are you, Wassail costume?" Zoey mused, eyeing the stack and hoping for a Wassail label to accompany the Christmas labels.

Even though she was in the attic, Zoey heard the knock at the front door before it opened and then shut. "Hello? Zoey?"

Jake.

*Oh, crap, what am I going to say to him? Do I apologize or wait for him to apologize? Should I wait and see if he's still angry?*

"Zoey? It's me, Jake," he called out, his voice drawing nearer. He climbed the stairs from the ground floor to the second story. Soon he would see the ladder to the attic, and he'd know where she was.

"I'm in the attic," Zoey called, wishing she didn't feel so nervous.

*Don't be lazy with your relationships, Zoey. He's been a good friend helping with the repairs on the house. He screwed up, sure, but forgiveness is important.*

The wooden ladder creaked as he climbed. Zoey first saw the back of his head and how red his ears were from being out in the cold. When he turned and spotted her by the wall of boxes, his green eyes were big like a heart-melting puppy.

"I was wrong, Zoey. I don't know how I let myself get so carried away. Stepping back and looking at my actions from your point of view, I wouldn't blame you if you kicked me out in the snow. You were right, completely right. I should have asked you before I started writing the article. I definitely should have asked you before I opened up the box with the letters and journals."

A clump of snow dropped from his hair onto his chest, wetting the ugly Christmas sweater inside his open coat. He paused and dusted more white flakes from his shiny black hair, changing his weight from his right foot to his left.

"Can you ever forgive me, Zoey?"

"Yeah, I mean, yes. Of course, I can forgive you.

Will you forgive me for freaking out so much? I mean, I still wish you would've asked, but I shouldn't have yelled like that."

Jake shook his head. "No way, you should have yelled. You were right to yell at me. I earned it."

"Well, I'm still very sorry that I spoke to you that way. I know you would have respected my feelings if I shared them with you; there was no reason to lose control."

"Either way, you were right. Can we hug it out? I'm just so grateful for the opportunity to be here, and I'm sorry I offended you. Truly."

Zoey waved a hand at him, figuring he was joking, but he approached her and held his hands out for a hug. "Oh, you're serious, sure." Surprisingly, when his arms wrapped around her and squeezed her, the awkward feelings she had vanished, and the weight of their fight melted away like the snow on his sweater.

"Now that that's out of the way, tell me what you're doing up here. Can I help?"

"I'm looking for the costume Grandma Matilda wore every year to the Wassail parade. It's probably in one of these Christmas boxes."

Jake scratched his chin, which Zoey was beginning

131

to recognize as one of his nervous tells.

"What?" she asked, giving him a nudge with her elbow.

"Well, earlier when I was all carried away and not thinking, I found a box in the front closet that I thought was the box of letters and everything. Once I pulled it down off the shelf, I spotted the word *Wassail* written on top." His cheeks were flushed already from the cold, but the way he averted his green eyes let Zoey know he was embarrassed to have to admit to further snooping.

Zoey couldn't help but laugh at his apparent nerves. "Hey, I'm glad you saw it. If you hadn't, I'd have been digging through all these Christmas boxes."

"Your Grandma Matilda must have loved Christmastime. There are a lot of boxes here."

Zoey nodded, smiling as she pictured Grandma Matilda's face when she would look at the inn after she completed the last of the decorating. "She did love Christmas. She would start decorating the day after Thanksgiving, and she'd sing Christmas Carols while she strung the lights on the house. Everyone in town came by during the holiday season to see how she decorated because she always went all out."

Zoey sighed as she thought about how this

Christmas would be the first time in over five decades that the Snapdragon Inn would be bare of Christmas décor.

"What do you think about putting up some lights?" Jake asked, rubbing his hands together. "We've got plenty of supplies to use."

"I think that's a great idea, and my grandma would love it." Zoey bit her lower lip to keep from smiling too big. "So would I." She stepped forward to open one of the boxes, but Jake touched her elbow to get her attention again.

"You might want to double-check and make sure the costume is in the box downstairs and that it fits. I don't want to make you late for the parade. Since you agreed to lead the ponies, I've heard nothing but how excited everyone is that you'll be participating in the parade."

Zoey nodded with a small smile curving her lips. It was nice to know that some people were excited she was participating.

"I'll get started on the lights; I mean, if you don't mind? I can wait if you'd prefer." Jake was already leaning toward the boxes but stopped himself, so he was frozen at a seventy-degree angle.

"No, I don't mind if you want to decorate for Christmas. These boxes are all fine for you to open."

Jake grinned and then she lost him to the mystery of what each Christmas box contained. He might as well have been opening presents under the tree he seemed so excited. Zoey left him to appease his curiosity and jogged down the stairs until she reached the ground floor.

In the front hall closet, she found a box labeled *Wassail* just as Jake had said. *All right, let's see what we've got here.* As soon as she pulled back the flaps of the box, Zoey caught a whiff of the apple-cinnamon body spray Grandma Matilda always wore during the Christmas holiday.

There were beautiful memories triggered by the smell, making all those memories seem so recent. Zoey lifted the red cloak trimmed with white faux fur and hugged it close. She inhaled the scent and all the bittersweet moments came back to life as she did.

The thick cloak was so soft that Zoey didn't hesitate to slip it on. It felt like her grandma was hugging her as she wore the cloak, and she wondered under what circumstance she would be convinced to take it off.

Next, she retrieved a black top hat, no doubt worn

when she drove the sleigh. Under the top hat, however, was a red Santa hat that matched the cloak perfectly. Inside the pocket of the cloak, she found white gloves. There was even a pair of black boots with white fur trim, and since she and Grandma Matilda wore the same size shoes, she knew they would fit.

While the cloak and boots were both gorgeous, Zoey was most pleased to find the fleece-lined red and white plaid leggings and the lovely, thick, white cable-knit sweater. Thanks to Grandma Matilda, Zoey was not only going to get to dress well, but she was also going to be warm.

After seeing how excited Jake was to decorate, Zoey was sure he was going to get carried away. She wanted to help him with the decorating, at least until she had to leave for the parade. With that in mind, Zoey took the Wassail box up to her room and changed into the costume. While there, she brushed out her hair and retouched her makeup.

There was a sort of joyful excitement in the air when she left her room to find Jake. Perhaps the Christmas spirit had found a way to warm her heart, which felt like a miracle with all that had been going on.

Zoey found Jake just beyond the tall stack of boxes

on the porch. One thing she had to say for Jake was that once he set out to do something, he didn't waste any time getting to it. He was climbing a ladder with bulging pockets full of light clips and a long string of lights wound like a wheel over his shoulder.

"Here you are, I thought I'd at least be able to help you bring down some boxes. Did you test the lights on that strand already, too?"

Jake looked at her from his stance halfway up the ladder and would have slipped off if he hadn't managed to catch himself. "Wow, Zoey, you look great." Jake's brilliant green eyes ran over her in the costume as his smile grew. "Christmas really agrees with you."

"Yeah? Well, then I better start scouting myself out a Santa Claus."

"That's not a bad idea," Mr. Bradshaw said as he trudged through the snow from his place. He was carrying a ladder on his shoulders as well. "I know there are quite a few single men in town who would love to play Santa to your Mrs. Claus." He chuckled as he came to a stop next to the porch. "I been helping Matilda hang lights the last five years or so, and I thought you might like some help."

Zoey nodded with a smile though she was squinting

from the bright sunlight bouncing off the pristine white snow. "That'd be great, but I don't want to make you late for the parade."

"If we work together, we could knock this job out fast and still have time to get downtown to help with the final preparations before the parade."

*Help with final preparations? Be surrounded by people who are likely to keep telling me what they think I should do? I don't think so.*

"Let's do it," Jake said.

Zoey got to work testing the next strand of lights while the two men began to string up the line that Jake held. Between the three of them, they got the roof over the porch lit all the way around the house so that every side glowed with red, green, and white lights. Jake got the idea that while Zoey was wrapping the lights around the posts and balustrade, he and Mr. Bradshaw should wrap the spire while they were up top putting up the remaining rooftop lights.

It was going to be tricky with snow on the roof, but the men were too excited to listen to Zoey when she cautioned them. Since the two were set to keep going, Zoey decided to wrap the shrubbery in the front yard so she could keep an eye on her Christmas elves decorating her rooftop.

Zoey recognized Maybell's curly blond and silver hair when she pulled into the driveway. She probably should have been surprised to see Maybell show up out of the blue, but she wasn't. Maybell hopped out of her car and started singing "The Twelve Days of Christmas" on her happy march to Zoey's side.

"This is just beautiful. Was it your idea to wrap the rooftop like that?" Maybell asked.

"No, I was worried about them slipping, but they're being careful. It's going to be pretty. I think Grandma Matilda would've loved that touch."

Maybell put her arm around Zoey and gave her a comforting hug. "I know she's watching you, just tickled pink that you've stopped everything you were busy doing to decorate the house."

Zoey nodded, knowing that if Grandma Matilda did have the ability to watch her, she would be delighted to see the lights going up. Looking back, there wasn't a single Christmas Zoey could recall where the holiday went undecorated.

"Did you find her sleigh and reindeer for the lawn?" Maybell asked.

"No, but I don't think they will be in any of those

boxes. They're big but not large enough to fit a sleigh."

Maybell shook her head, and her curls bounced. "No, it'll be in the loft in the garage, I helped Matilda put them up there a few years back. I'll get them. I have time to lend you a hand for a little bit."

"You don't have to, Maybell."

"Oh, honey, I want to."

Mr. Bradshaw started down the ladder, so Zoey left the project she was working and hurried to hold it for him.

"We're going to get these plugged in and then we'll wrap the railings with garland and hang the mistletoe."

"We?" Zoey asked following him up onto the porch.

He nodded with a laugh that could have come from old Saint Nick himself. "Yes, we. Look up the lane, my dear. The cavalry is coming."

Cars pulled in the driveway stacking up one behind the other. There were people she hadn't seen in years along with people she'd only met in passing arriving to offer their help.

Shocked beyond words, Zoey found herself speechless as the neighbors and friends of Grandma Matilda joyfully put themselves to work.

"How did you know we were putting up Christmas lights?" Zoey asked Gertrude, catching her as she got out of her car.

"Thomas Crowley lives farther up the mountain. You remember him, don't you, dear? Well, anyway," she continued without waiting for Zoey's response, "he saw you all getting to work. He put the call out that Snapdragon Inn was getting all decked out for Christmas! We all know that lots of helping hands make heavy work light, so here we are."

Zoey nodded, blinking away the moisture that came to her eyes. "It's so nice that so many people want to help."

"Well, my dear, it is nice, but we think it's ever so nice that you're decorating at all. You've had your hands quite full with all the repairs the place requires. We would have understood if you didn't decorate. But I'll admit, it was going to be quite hard on all of us to see Matilda's house dark for Christmas. This is boosting all our spirits. So, thank you, Zoey."

*They miss her, too. How did I not see that?*

Zoey wrapped her arms around Gertrude and squeezed. A little squeak came out of Gertrude before she hugged Zoey back. Knowing they shared a love for

140

Matilda made Zoey feel like her tiny family had just grown, and suddenly, she wasn't so alone.

"Your Grandma Matilda was so proud of you. I know she still is," Gertrude said as Zoey stepped back. "Now let's get the decorations up. I've got to check the wreaths for the parade still."

She and Gertrude set to tying the wreaths on the balustrade with the weather-resistant red ribbon making pretty bows. Men and young boys shoveled the driveway and sidewalks.

The sleigh and reindeer were set up by Maybell and Corey, who used rebar poles to lift the sleigh off the ground so that it would appear like Santa was landing his sleigh once the sun went down.

"Would you like lanterns lining the front walkway or candy canes?" Jake asked, holding up an example of each for Zoey.

"I think lanterns," Zoey said. "What do you think?"

Jake set the oversized, red-and-white-striped, plastic candy cane back into its box. "Lanterns, for sure."

"Oh, you see that?" Gertrude whispered in a conspiratorial manner. "Look." She gestured out toward Maybell, who was handing another man the mallet she'd been using on the rebar. "That's Lincoln Ingle. You're too young to remember this, but those two used to be quite an item."

"Looks like they may be rekindling that old flame," Jake said, having drawn closer to hear the gossip.

*Men really are so much gossipier than women.*

"What?" Jake asked, giving Zoey a sheepish smile. "Hey, I hear Maybell isn't the only one with an old flame here. Corey Finch was a boyfriend of yours, wasn't he?"

"How in the world do you know about that?" Zoey laughed.

"Mr. Bradshaw mentioned it when Corey arrived. He said your Grandma Matilda never passed up an opportunity to tell him how great you were doing in New York. You gonna go take a stroll down memory lane?"

Zoey shook her head. "That wasn't anything serious. We were still just kids."

"Good," Jake said.

Zoey and Gertrude both looked at him then, and his ears burned red as he blushed.

"I just meant, you're already so busy. Plus, he's a lawyer. You don't need a serious lawyer type."

"Mmm-hmmm, someone more artsy and fun would suit you better," Gertrude agreed.

Zoey shook her head with a laugh. "Thank

goodness you two figured that out for me."

"I'm going to go plug in the lights and make sure the roof is finished before I start with the lanterns," Jake said.

Zoey already knew what was coming as Gertrude watched him go. "That young man thinks quite a lot of you," Gertrude said. "He's not bad to look at either."

"Gertrude, he's a coworker of mine. We're just friends."

"Sounds like a great place to start to me." Her brown eyes looked just as mischievous as her grin.

Zoey laughed. "You're the town's cupid, aren't you, Gertrude?"

"Don't I wish. I can see a relationship disaster coming a hundred miles away, but nobody bothers to ask me." She nodded toward Corey. "He's nice enough, but he's still recovering from his divorce. Plus, I agree he's too serious for you; he'd stress you out. Jake, on the other hand, needs a strong woman like you."

"Thanks, Gertrude," Zoey said, since she wasn't sure what else she could say. She hoped that agreeing with her would stop her from continuing.

Gertrude had always been so quiet, but her brown eyes were sage, and her mind was quick. The look she gave Zoey let her know she hadn't fooled Gertrude in the least. "The lights are on. Why don't you go help Jake with the lanterns so you can get out in the yard and get a look at the lights?"

"But we're not done tying the bows."

"We've only got three left, and I will manage them just fine. Go on," Gertrude said, giving Zoey a little push.

Zoey was a little afraid that if she didn't start moving, Gertrude would recruit help from Maybell, and unlike Gertrude, Maybell was not quiet about anything. So, she gave Gertrude a nod and followed Jake, who was unpacking the lanterns from the packaging.

"Your Grandma Matilda took excellent care of her decorations. These are the original boxes," Jake said when Zoey reached his side.

"She loved Christmas, so that doesn't surprise me. Can I help you with these?"

Jake handed her one of the boxes. "Sure."

"The lights look great. You and Mr. Bradshaw did an awesome job. Thank you."

"Don't thank me yet, Zoey. I figure you're going to have to take all of this stuff down and we're making a lot of work for you."

Zoey shrugged. "Not until after the holidays are over and besides, it's worth it."

"The people in this town are pretty amazing, showing up to help you decorate this place. I can see why your Grandma Matilda enjoyed living here. I mean, besides owning this incredible house in this picturesque place. It's just refreshing to see people come together like this."

"I agree. I can't believe it. I certainly didn't expect all this. The Snapdragon Inn looks astonishing, so much like I remember it when it's decorated like this."

Jake was watching her, she realized, and she lowered her gaze back to the box in her hands.

"Guess I better stop gabbing and help get these lanterns up."

"Yeah, me, too. I hear they're all heading to town for pre-parade setup. Are we going to that?"

Zoey used the little rubber mallet in the box to tap down the shepherd's crook post for the lantern as she considered his question. "I wasn't going to, if I'm honest, but now? I don't think I want to miss it. Weird, huh?"

"Not at all. I've got the same feeling. Maybe you're contagious." He grinned.

"Me? No, it's you. Definitely you."

He laughed as he straightened, standing closer than she anticipated and yet she didn't have the urge to step back.

"Are you warm enough?" he asked, his green eyes looking into hers.

"Yeah, this cloak is great."

He nodded, tucking it in closer around Zoey. "There's a storm coming; just wanted to make sure."

# CHAPTER 17

**Matilda Dunn's Diary**
**December 22, 1966**

A bunch of people from work decided to go to the winter bonfire at Quechee Gorge after our shift ended. I knew I wasn't going to be able to sleep because Joseph was due to come back for winter break the next day, so I decided to go, too.

There were about six other people there when my group of eight arrived. Wallace was there at closing and decided to tag along with us. Ricky Bradshaw had his guitar and started playing, even though with the drop in temperature as the sun set, he had to stop a few times and retune it.

More people started showing up, and after Ricky ran out of holiday songs to play, he started playing some swing tunes, and that got people dancing. I was clapping along, thinking that Ricky was much better at the guitar than the guys who played at the town festival last fall, when Wallace grabbed my wrist and pulled me out where couples were dancing.

I tried to tell him I'm not much of a dancer.

He looked at me side-eyed and told me not to be shy. He mumbled something about how he heard Joe and I were taking a break.

I shouldn't have been surprised that Wallace had that information, since word spreads quickly in Woodstock. I told him we were taking a temporary step back, but we're still together.

"It's just one dance," Wallace said. I think it was the way he said it that made me feel like I was silly in resisting. I started dancing with him, and the heads started turning. As soon as we started dancing, I wanted to stop, but it was too late. Even if we did stop—even if I did walk away—everyone at the bonfire would be gossiping about the dance the next day.

I told myself not to panic. Joseph wouldn't care if I danced one dance. He'd listen to me when I told him it was nothing. He knew me and knew he was the man I loved. Once I decided that, I loosened up and danced with a smile on my face as I told Wallace how Joseph would be arriving the next day.

Wallace said that he hoped I got time with my friend since he would most likely be spending the holiday with his family. Wallace wasn't wrong about that, but even if I got just ten minutes with Joseph, it would make me so happy. The idea of really missing someone seems like something that a strong young woman like me should be able to cope with.

I was genuinely missing someone. I mean, really, really missing them the way I've been missing Joseph is nothing at all like the concept of missing someone. My heart has ached to the point there were times I wanted it just to stop beating it hurt so badly. I pushed on, and I tried to keep moving and working to ease the symptom. As I went on acting like I was not in agony, my heart felt like it had grown into a colossal bowling ball in my chest. It felt hollow, cold, empty, and so very heavy.

Maybe that was why I felt that even a handful of minutes would be enough. I was desperate to see Joseph. I couldn't wait to hug him and hear him laugh. To have his eyes meet mine and feel that connection was what I longed for.

Wallace, with his negative way of looking at my situation with Joseph, went on talking about how I deserved a man who was present in my life. I started to tease him about his dancing skills to get him to change the topic, and it worked. He pulled a few moves that were silly and had us both laughing.

The song ended, and we all started clapping for Ricky. Then, almost immediately, the clapping died away, and I looked around as I continued to clap, wondering why everyone else had stopped.

Before I saw him, I think I felt that he was near because my heart started fluttering in my chest. I was bundled up in my winter coat, but I could still feel that chill of excitement that flitted down my spine. Then I saw him.

Joseph.

My Joseph.

I couldn't believe my eyes. He wasn't supposed to have arrived until the next day. It was why I'd gone out to the bonfire in the first place. How did he find me? How did he know where I was? It wasn't like me to go to the bonfire.

Joseph, dressed in a heather-gray coat cut like a suit jacket, appeared so much more man than boy as he stood at the edge of the forest clearing. His eyes were bright blue, intense, and heated. Joseph's blond hair shined with the light of the fire catching the lightest streaks.

I watched him, waiting to see if he'd be cross with me for dancing with someone else.

His breath came out in thick foggy puffs of air in the cold. I couldn't tell if he was angry. I was afraid he might be upset, but I was just so happy to see him. I smiled at him even before he started across the distance between us.

I realized he'd probably seen me dancing with Wallace, and I thought that was why Joseph wasn't smiling. The expression on his face was so severe, so very solemn.

Even if Joseph was upset, I knew I could explain it to him, and he would understand. At least I hoped he would.

I opened my mouth to tell him Wallace was just a friend, but I didn't get the chance. Right there, in front of everyone, Joseph pulled me into his strong arms and kissed me for what felt like the whole world to see.

I don't even know when my arms wrapped around him, but when he pulled back, everyone had started clapping again, and Ricky started playing another song. This one was a slow song, and Joseph continued to hold me tight. It's so hard to explain but as we danced, we just looked at each other. We didn't say anything—at least not aloud.

We didn't need words because I saw his love for me in his eyes and he saw mine for him. I felt invincible in his arms, like there was nothing we couldn't do or get through as we danced, holding each other under a sparkling blanket of stars. I certainly didn't want the dance to end, but of course, it did.

Afterward, I introduced Joseph to Wallace,

and Joseph acted like the good man I knew him to be. He shook hands with Wallace and put his arm around me, saying that he was always happy to meet one of his girlfriend's friends.

Wallace left after that, and I doubt I'll see him again at the café. I don't think he thought Joseph would come back for me. I'd had my doubts a few times myself. When Joseph arrived that night, however, I realized how ridiculous those fears had been.

Joseph told me how he left right after the final exams because he needed so much to see me. I knew just what he meant. After we danced a while and visited with a few friends, Joseph and I left the bonfire and headed to the Victorian.

There was something on Joseph's mind, I could see that, and I would have been nervous if he hadn't kissed me like that in front of so many people. Joseph is a private person, not one to give public displays of affection, and so I knew that no matter what he'd say, it was going to be okay. Joseph and I could get through anything.

Joseph closed the door with us inside and kissed me up against the door. I could've gotten lost in that kiss, and I think we would have if we hadn't heard Ricky strumming his guitar as he returned to his home; he didn't live far from the Victorian.

Being the gentleman that he is, Joseph stepped back, holding onto my hand as he did. I was glad he didn't break contact altogether. He admitted that he was jealous when he saw me dancing with Wallace. I apologized, but he told me I didn't need to apologize. He said when I smiled at him, he knew that I loved him still and that was all he'd needed to know.

I thought he was going to tell me all about the things he'd been doing at school. Instead, he took both of my hands in his and said, "I've made up my mind, Matilda. I know what I want."

My heart started pounding so hard in my

ears. I was afraid I wouldn't be able to hear what he was going to say, and that was terrible. I told him to wait a second so my heart would slow down. After all, what he would say was going to impact what my life with him would be like. I didn't know if he was going to continue school for another few years, perhaps changing his major since law wasn't for him. Would we have to be apart for years? Months?

Joseph must have decided he'd waited long enough because he said he was finished with Stanford and he was dropping out.

I asked him if it was because I was dancing with Wallace. I couldn't help asking him that question because I wanted his decision to be his own and not because of me.

Joseph kissed my fingers as his thumbs made circles over the top of my hands. He said he made the decision last week. He said he knew after he finished his finals for the quarter, he was coming home for good.

At first, I was ecstatic at his news. He'd made a decision, and he was going to take a stand against his parents. But as soon as I thought about him standing against his parents to tell them he wouldn't be returning, I was afraid for him. I still am.

Joseph was reassuring. He told me that he would be fine no matter what they said because he knew without a doubt that Stanford wasn't what he wanted.

He seemed so sure of himself, and I believe him—it's just, his parents are such hard, cold people when it comes to getting what they want.

I don't want him to be hurt by them, but I realize that this is something he must do on his own. Still, there is no telling what they are going to do when he tells them. I pray they don't sign him up to be drafted. Only last week, I heard his father say to the pharmacist it was what he'd do if Joseph didn't finish school.

Joseph and I talked about what he would like to do instead, and I was surprised to hear him say that we should fix up the Victorian. I always talked about doing that, but instead of just fixing up an oversized house, I thought we could do so much more with it. He suggested we repair the Victorian with a mind of making it into a bed and breakfast.

For a little while, we got carried away talking about all the different things we could do to the Victorian, and it was so wonderful. I could see that it was what he wanted, too.

Now I am stuck waiting and praying for everything to go okay with Joseph and his family. I haven't seen him or heard from him all day. I was so nervous at work today. I dropped a tray of food and spilled hot coffee on myself twice. I hope I hear from Joseph soon...

# CHAPTER 18

After such an incredible show of support from so many in Woodstock, Zoey wasn't going to miss her chance to return the favor. As soon as she doubled up her socks to better fit Grandma Matilda's boots, Zoey climbed aboard the Range Rover and headed to the staging area.

There were still two hours before the big Wassail parade would begin, but people were already working frantically to get everything in its place and at its best for showtime.

Because of the warm showing of love and support Zoey had received when so many showed up at the inn to help, Zoey assumed there would be the same feeling when she arrived to help with the parade. She should have known better. Rosemary wasn't up at the inn spreading contention the way she was at the staging center.

People appeared shocked to see Zoey there. Ernest's huge mouth dropped open so much his gum fell out of his mouth.

For an instant, Zoey considered retreating. It would be so easy to hop back in the Rover and return to the inn and let someone else lead the biting ponies in the parade. Or even leave and then return to play the part she'd agreed to play.

Instead, Zoey decided to ignore the fact people were staring and that she was already blushing. Straightening her shoulders, she tossed her hair over her shoulder and approached Stella Murphy, who was one of Rosemary's minions but who also was balancing armloads of supplies.

"Let me help you with those. Where are we taking them?" Zoey asked with a smile on her face.

"You want to help?"

Zoey took one of the oversized toolboxes from Stella. "Of course, I want to help. Where are we taking these?"

It was quiet, uncomfortably quiet, in fact. Stella swallowed what must have been shock because the dumbfounded look she'd been wearing was replaced with a bright-eyed smile. "That's wonderful, Zoey! We'd love to have your help. Thank you," Stella gushed.

The stunned onlookers started smiling, too, and some of them even began to nod their agreement.

Zoey kept her smile in place and followed Stella with the big toolbox over to the makeshift stalls where the horses and ponies were being held. Inside the toolbox were brushes for the animals, oils, bows, and all kinds of things.

"Would you like to help me get them ready?" Stella asked.

"Sure," Zoey answered before she could chicken out. It had been quite a while since she was in contact with horses.

Stella handed her one of the brushes. "We're going to give their backs a nice once over before we get to putting the ribbons in their manes."

Zoey watched Stella get started on the white horse with the gray patches before she approached the chestnut brown horse with the black mane. Zoey ran her hand over the shoulder and back of the beautiful, powerful horse. "You're a big, beautiful horse, aren't you?" Zoey asked as the animal looked over at her. His body was warm and velvety smooth, but what eased her nerves most were his big, brown, kind eyes. "Last year, Grandma Matilda drove one of the sleighs for the parade, and maybe you were one of the horses. She had a gentle hand, so you would've liked her."

The smile over the shoulder that Stella gave Zoey made her realize she was talking to the horse, and she laughed at herself.

"You've got a calming way about you, Zoey. Matilda was just the same. My horses always loved getting attention from her."

"He likes the sound of your voice, too," Jake said, surprising Zoey with his presence and taking a picture of her surprised face all at once. "Can't blame him there." Jake grinned.

Zoey cocked an eyebrow at him. "I thought you were going to do a few more things around the inn before coming down?"

"I was. Then I saw you leave, and I thought I'd better get over here and see what kind of trouble I could get myself into."

Zoey stiffened involuntarily as Ernest came to stand next to Jake. "'Bout time I see you pitching in, Mr. Ward. We see Zoey working and coming to town for supplies plenty. She sure isn't the kind to shy away from hard work. Reminds us of Matilda, she does." Ernest nodded toward Zoey, and she found herself giving him a nod back.

"I will endeavor to make myself more useful," Jake said easily.

Ernest tipped his black top hat with the mistletoe sitting at the base and then gave Jake a poke in the ribs with his elbow. "See that you do."

Jake watched Ernest as he strolled away with his thumbs hooked in the pockets of his red, oversized suit jacket. "He's an interesting one, isn't he?" Jake asked, shaking his head.

"Yeah, he is. One of many."

"Seems to approve of you though, that's got to feel nice. Right?"

Zoey laughed as she shook her head and ran the brush over the horse's back. "Approve is probably too strong a word for Ernest. I think he's in favor of me working and helping with the parade."

"Oh, no, you just got the nod of approval. Ernest

doesn't give those out willy-nilly, my dear," Stella put in.

Jake's smile grew with the deepening shade of pink coloring Zoey's cheeks. "You see?"

"Heads up, kids, here comes the head angel," Stella warned before ducking her head down as she continued to work.

Rosemary, dressed in a white dress with silver wings fanned out behind her, was making a beeline right toward Zoey and Jake, so there was no time to duck away or prepare for the 'head angel's' arrival.

"You came. I was all but certain you weren't going to fit us into your schedule. Then again, Mr. Ward did mention wanting to photograph the event." Rosemary struck a pose, turning to the side, leaning backward slightly and pouting her painted red lips. Her tight red curls made her head appear twice its usual size and coupled with her iridescent eye makeup and red boots, made it difficult both to look at her or look away.

"I'll wait and take pictures when the parade is underway," Jake said, realizing after several long drawn out moments that she was waiting for her picture to be taken.

Rosemary's nostrils flared as she relaxed her stance and turned her attention to Zoey. "You're early, that's unexpected as well. No doubt Maybell drug you out, hmm?"

"No. I drove myself, and I'm earlier than you suggested for obvious reasons. I'm also dressed, so I won't need whatever costume you had in mind."

Rosemary's shoulders bobbed a bit like she was getting revved up to give Zoey a piece of her mind.

"It's great that you're so heavily involved in the parade, and that so many of the kind people of Woodstock don't mind taking orders from you, Rosemary. However, I won't be one who requires your directions."

Rosemary's shoulders stilled, and her eyes widened. "Excuse me. I was only trying to help!"

"Please don't help me. Don't help me by speaking to my attorney and trying to direct what I'll do with my childhood home or by notifying the rumor mill of my feelings since you're not privy to them."

"Are you hearing this?" Rosemary asked Stella.

Stella nodded. "I am, and it sounds to me like you owe Matilda's granddaughter an apology."

"Look," Zoey said, knowing that she wasn't quite ready to swallow a fake apology. "If your intentions were well-meaning, it's a shame they didn't come off that way. I've let you know where I stand, and I hope that you'll respect my wishes. Other than that, I wish you a happy Wassail Weekend."

Rosemary continued to stare with her mouth ajar, so Zoey turned back to the horse and resumed brushing him. She thought she'd be uptight and angry after speaking her mind to Rosemary, but she found that she was relieved, instead.

"Good for you, honey," Stella said, giving Zoey a wink. "Rosemary will run you right over if you don't stand up to her. Now that you have, I expect you two will get along quite well."

"You never know," Zoey said, smiling as the horse leaned into the brush strokes. "He loves this, doesn't he? What's his name?"

Stella smiled. "Freedom Banner, but I call him Banner. Matilda favored him as well."

Zoey nodded, remembering Jake, but he was no longer standing beside her. She spotted him helping to hoist barrels of candy into one of the carriages. Zoey also noticed the huddle of women, just beyond him, watching him work. If he wanted to, it was clear he could pick himself up a few girlfriends in Woodstock as his group of admirers continued to grow.

"Banner is all brushed out. Shall I start brushing another horse for you? I'm not sure how to put the ribbon into his mane," Zoey confessed.

"Oh, it's not too tricky. Just follow what I do with Polly here," Stella said, handing Zoey a mess of red and white ribbons. Zoey didn't want to let Stella down, so she observed, and with the help of a stepping stool and Banner's patience, Zoey managed to imitate the weaving plait Stella put on Polly.

From there, Zoey found herself recruited to help with face paint for Santa's elves. Tabitha was the third elf to sit in the makeup chair for painted-on freckles and oversized eyelashes. "Zoey, look at you all grown up and sophisticated. It's so good to see you," Tabitha said flashing her gorgeous smile, the same one that won her Homecoming Queen their senior year in high school.

"It's nice to see you, too, Tabitha. How are you doing, anyway?" Zoey asked as she got to work painting the fake eyelashes.

Tabitha sighed. "Well, Brandon and I got divorced last year. The dating scene is pretty scarce around here for our age group, but no way in heck I'm leaving Woodstock. It's home, you know?"

Zoey nodded.

"Your Jake is quite a looker."

"He is very handsome, but he's not mine. We're just friends," Zoey said, though she was thinking of the way he'd tucked her cloak around her back at the inn.

Tabitha's big smile returned. "Oh, sweetie, he's working his cute butt off helping you with the inn, I hear, and today with the parade. Men don't just work for the fun of it. I think he's got a crush on you."

Zoey cocked an eyebrow at Tabitha because she didn't intend to let herself get pulled into a gab session about Jake. Just a few hours earlier, Gertrude had tried shoving him at her, but Zoey wasn't the kind to rush anything or jump to conclusions.

"Well, I mean, I heard when Corey asked around that you said Jake was just a friend, so I asked him out. I figured you wouldn't mind since you two are just friends."

The pang of annoyance Zoey felt toward Tabitha at that moment was unreasonable, and she told herself as much before she responded, "Yeah? Are you two going to the open house?"

"No. He turned me down flat. He said he was here with you." Tabitha watched Zoey for her response, and when she didn't get one, she added, "And I'm not the only woman he told that to."

Zoey tried not to smile and failed. "Well, he's here working on an article. He probably just doesn't want to mix work with play, as they say."

"He doesn't want to mess up his chances with you is what he doesn't want. Take my word for it— he's here for you."

That made Zoey's stomach stir with surging electric energy that she wasn't sure what to do with. "You're all set," Zoey said to Tabitha.

"Thanks. Hey, I hope you stick around. I mean, I know you don't have to, but it would be so great to hang out sometime. We have so much to catch up on."

Zoey returned the warm smile Tabitha gave her as she remembered hanging around with Tabitha back in the day. Tabitha was still a straightforward, fun person. She'd replace Brandon soon enough, no doubt about that.

Someone started calling, "Places, everyone. Get into your proper places. The parade is about to begin. Twelve minutes, only twelve minutes."

Zoey returned the paints to Maybell and found her place leading a pretty white pony with big red bows on its mane and tail.

"You look great," Jake said, pausing to snap a

picture of them.

"I don't think Birdseye will want pictures of me all over Woodstock." Zoey tried to laugh, but it came out higher pitched than she would have liked. "Did you get a chance to take some pictures of all those foreboding clouds outside? I hope the storm doesn't start during the parade."

Jake's smile made that tingly feeling in her stomach gain momentum, and she knew she was blushing again.

*Seriously, Zoey? You don't have enough on your plate to deal with? You're going to indulge in your crush on Jake, now?*

"Actually, it has already started coming down, but it's not too heavy yet. Be careful out there."

"Seven minutes," Maybell announced as she dashed by them holding onto her hat as the doors opened and the wind pushed inside the barn.

Zoey held onto her own hat as the parade began.

With Christmas music playing cheerfully, it wasn't so bad marching, even with the random gusts of wind and giant snowflakes swirling through the air.

There was a big turnout for the parade, and it was such a boost to see so many smiling familiar faces both in the parade and watching it. Friends from the past called to Zoey from the sidelines, and she squinted to see them through the thickening snow haze.

The high school marching band playing "Jingle Bells" kept Zoey and everyone else in the parade moving at a good pace, so when one of the horses stopped walking, Zoey took notice as the dancing elves passed up the silver-winged angel on the horse.

*What is Rosemary doing?*

"Come on, Banner, come on," Zoey heard Rosemary saying as she drew closer.

"She must have dug her heels in," one of the men in the carriage following Zoey was saying to someone else. "That horse isn't going to move an inch for her now."

Zoey bit her lower lip.

*It's not right to laugh. I know it isn't. I'm not going to laugh.*

Rosemary turned around in the saddle as she searched for someone to help her. The look on her face was one Zoey hadn't expected. Rosemary had streaks through her makeup where tears fell, and she looked so defeated.

A massive gust of wind caught hold of her wings just then, and she was nearly unseated, adding fear to her already weighted expression. Zoey glanced around,

171

figuring someone would trot up to help Rosemary, but as she looked around, it was clear that everyone in the parade was doing their best to keep hold of their displays to keep them from blowing away.

Zoey groaned inwardly as she led the pony to the back of the carriage that had been following her. "Can I tie her on to the carriage? I'm gonna go see if I can get Banner walking."

"Sure. Good idea," the driver called back.

Zoey handed the rope to one of the passengers to tie off and then jogged back around to the front and approached Banner. "Hey, there, Banner. What's the matter?" Zoey asked, running a careful hand down his face and taking hold of the lead.

"He won't move. I keep telling him to go," Rosemary said from his back.

"You hold onto the horn, and I'll take the lead. Maybe he'll walk for me," Zoey said, keeping her voice calm and even. Rosemary let go of the reins. "Banner, let's you and me take a walk. All right?" Zoey asked, continuing to pet him and speak in what she hoped was a soothing tone.

When Banner leaned into her touch, she smiled, ignoring the blast of icy wind. "We're almost done. Just

one more block. You ready, Banner? Here we go."
Walking to the front and off to the left side, Zoey prayed
Banner would cooperate with her.

*Come on, Banner, don't make us stand out here in
the storm with Rosemary Billings!*

People on the sidelines cheered as Banner allowed
her to lead him, and she smiled through her chattering
teeth, waving to them. If it hadn't been for Grandma
Matilda's warm Wassail ensemble, Zoey was sure she
would have become a human popsicle before they
finished the first leg of the parade route.

The parade had forged ahead when Banner took his
stand, and so Zoey walked as quickly as she safely could
to catch up, but when they did, it was at the endpoint of
the parade and people were dispersing, packing up their
floats, loading the smaller animals into trailers, and
heading for cover.

Stella waved at Zoey, calling out to her, but it was
hard to hear her in the howling wind. Zoey spotted her
thankfully because of her waving hands and led Banner
to Stella's horse trailer.

"It'll take both of us to help Rosemary down," Stella
said once Zoey was close enough to hear her.

Zoey nodded, and the two of them worked together

173

to help Rosemary dismount, which proved especially tricky since she was quite stiff from the cold, and the wind wasn't giving them a break either.

Jake pulled alongside them in his Outlander. "Hop in. I'll give you a ride back to your car."

"You're a lifesaver, Jake," Zoey said and climbed into the back seat so she wouldn't have to run around the other side of the SUV.

"Rosemary? Rosemary? I can give you... Well, okay," Stella was saying, and Zoey felt resistance on the door as she started pulling it shut. Rosemary pulled it open and climbed into the back seat beside her.

Jake's green eyes widened a little as he looked at Zoey in the rearview mirror. Zoey shrugged, figuring Rosemary was too cold to care if she had to ride next to Zoey. Maybe she was furious with Stella and didn't want to ride with her after Banner refused to move for her.

Jake turned off the main road and began to backtrack toward the original staging area where the parade began.

"Ms. Larson... er... Zoey," Rosemary began, though she appeared to be talking to her hands. "I want to thank you for helping me with Stella's horse. There were so many people around, lots who I was surprised to see walk right on past me without trying to help. I can honestly say that the last person I thought was going to help me was you."

*Nice backhanded thank you, Rosemary.*

"Sure," Zoey said.

"I'm sorry, that didn't come out correctly. What I mean is, after my poor behavior, I wouldn't have blamed you if you had ignored my plight." Her voice shook a bit, and she dabbed at her eyes.

Zoey felt that hard section of her heart softening where Rosemary was concerned.

"There is no good reason for my bad behavior. I've just always lacked trust in letting people do what needs to be done. People around here let me be bossy, but they let me know when I go too far. At least, I hope they do. I went too far, not only that..." Rosemary trailed off, raising her gaze to meet Zoey's.

Zoey, in shock that she was getting an apology from Rosemary, stared back, seeing sincerity where she thought she'd find crocodile tears.

"I was unkind. There's just no call for that, and you didn't deserve it. It's not your fault Matilda's gone. I just miss her so much." Rosemary gulped as she folded her arms tightly across her chest.

She blinked and sniffed before continuing, probably attempting to keep her composure. "Today, you proved you're a far better woman than I am by helping out with the parade after I was so rude, and then by coming to my rescue. I do hope you decide to stay here because I think you'd be a great asset for us, but that's your choice, of course. Can you ever forgive me?"

Zoey nodded. "Yes, I forgive you, Rosemary. I miss her, too."

Rosemary burst into tears, hugging Zoey with a strength that Zoey wouldn't have believed her capable of. Caught off guard, Zoey's eyes bulged from the tight squeeze as she spotted Jake's huge, charming smile in the rearview mirror.

"Let's get you ladies into your vehicles. It's really coming down," Jake said after a few moments.

"Thank you," Rosemary said to Jake as she released Zoey. "I know I made a poor impression, but I hope you won't hold that against Woodstock, Mr. Ward."

Jake shook his head as he got out of the car and he said something, but with the wind, neither woman could decipher it. Zoey got out with Rosemary and held her arm to make sure she didn't fall as they trotted to Rosemary's car. Jake swept the snow from her windows with his sleeve as Rosemary got behind the wheel.

"Drive safely," Zoey said before closing the door for Rosemary.

Zoey turned to head to the Rover, but Jake caught her arm. "It's coming down harder by the second; let's come back for it tomorrow."

"Sounds good," Zoey yelled to be heard over the wind, and they hurried to the Outlander.

Zoey got in the passenger seat this time. Jake got in behind the wheel and drove carefully onto the main road. "This is coming down so thick, I can barely see three feet in front of us."

Zoey was aware and was glad he was going slow. It took three times as long to make it back to the Snapdragon, but when they did, it was just in time to see the Christmas lights go out as the severe weather cut the power.

# CHAPTER 19

"I'm sorry I didn't get a chance to get the generator looked at before this storm," Zoey apologized as she and Jake stacked wood in the fireplace.

"What? Don't be silly. This fire will do the trick."

Zoey laughed. "You say that now, but I don't know if you'll think so in a few hours when we're still snowed in, and there's no television or radio."

"We'll find entertainment, I'm sure." The fire, catching to the kindling, made orange lights dance over Jake's handsome face, and Zoey felt that surge of nervous energy return.

"I'll go find some candles. Grandma Matilda was

always good about keeping supplies like that on hand. I know she has some lanterns. I just have to remember where she kept them." She stood, telling herself to stop babbling.

Even though it was still early evening, there was only dim light coming through the windows because of the blizzard. Soon that, too, would fade, and the house would be dark.

"I'll go fetch more wood from the shed," Jake said with what might've been a shy smile. Somehow, it helped if he was feeling a little nervous, too.

Zoey set about finding candles, flashlights, and lanterns. She struck power outage supply gold when she checked the closet under the staircase. "Grandma Matilda, you sure knew how to prepare for these things," Zoey said, picking up the cast iron pot that could be used to cook over the fire.

The closet supplied them with two lanterns, candles, an oversized Sherpa blanket, and a dozen board games to choose from if conversation lulled and boredom set in. Zoey brought the supplies to the living room and then went to the kitchen.

There were so many lovely dishes given to them from the people of Woodstock. The quart of chicken noodle soup called out to Zoey, so she picked it up and the box of saltine crackers to go with it.

"Aw, yes, you read my mind," Jake said when she entered the living room with the food. "I'll go get bowls, spoons, and a ladle."

"It's a little early for them. We haven't even started warming the soup," Zoey laughed.

Jake nodded in agreement but was still headed toward the kitchen. "I know, but I'm starving," he exclaimed.

Using the poker, Zoey pulled forward the hook installed in the back of the fireplace and then used it again to hang the pot containing the soup. Jake returned with the other supplies he went for. He added another log to the fire, even though Zoey was pretty sure he did that so he could lean in close and smell the soup.

"I'm going to change into more comfortable clothes. You probably should, too. Your sweater looks like it got wet." Zoey said as she got up from the fireplace.

"Yeah, I guess I will. I bet the soup will heat up faster if I'm not staring at it, anyway."

It was still light enough they didn't need the lanterns or a candle. Jake stood aside to allow Zoey to climb the stairs first.

"So, just to be clear, when you say more comfortable, you mean what exactly?" Jake asked as they neared the top of the staircase.

"I mean dry, comfortable clothes. What do you mean, what do I mean?"

Jake laughed, and his ears were burning enough that she could see them in the low light of the upper hallway. "I just didn't want to get into pajamas, and you return in a pretty sweater and trousers or something."

"Oh, I see. I'm going to get in pajamas or thermals, maybe sweats. Does that help you?"

"Immensely," he said, and they both laughed.

Zoey went into her room and stripped out of the damp clothes. Earlier in the trip, she'd moved some of Grandma Matilda's warmer clothes into the closet in case she got cold, and this was the night to find something on the warmer side of things.

Somehow knowing that Jake was going to see her in whatever outfit she put on made it more challenging to settle on something. Zoey went through everything she had and then decided on a set of pale pink fleece pajamas. Her slippers were slim, yellow, and fuzzy.

Even though the cellphone signal was weak at the Snapdragon Inn, Zoey dug her mobile phone from the clothes she changed out of. She didn't have any intention of using the phone but did want to double-check to make sure it wasn't wet.

The little white number thirty-two inside the red bubble next to the text messages icon made her stomach tighten. Something had to be going on for there to be so many texts. Zoey opened the message screen. The first thing she noticed was that Celeste had left the bulk of the text messages. She opened Celeste's messages first.

Celeste: *Turns out we need a verbal confirmation from you.*

Celeste: *I'm referring to the opportunity of a lifetime, remember?*

Celeste: *Hello?*

Celeste: *Just a quick call is all we need.*

Celeste: *Are you getting any of these messages?*

Celeste: *If we don't get a call from you before midnight, the job will be offered to someone else.*

Celeste: *CALL, ZOEY!!!!!*

The rest of the messages from Celeste were a repeat of the information she'd already sent.

*Geez, Celeste. Pushy much?*

Zoey tapped the backward arrow and opened the messages from Kenzie.

K. Highsmith: *Zoey, this is Kenzie Highsmith. Celeste failed to inform you that to secure the promotion offer you'll need to give a verbal confirmation.*

K. Highsmith: *Frankly, I'm surprised I haven't received word from you thanking me for this opportunity at all.*

Zoey's eyes widened, her cheeks heating up as if she were being admonished in person by Kenzie. That woman set standards to be met that no one was aware of until they were being slapped for not meeting them.

*Don't let them rush you, Zoey,* she told herself but didn't feel reassured.

The remaining text messages were from her friend Megan.

Megan: *How could you not call and tell me you got offered Senior Lead Journalist?*

Megan: *I'm so happy for you.*

Megan: *You're taking the job, right?*

Megan: *Hello?*

Megan: *Right?*

Zoey clicked the button on the side of the phone to turn off the screen.

*No more pressure. I'm not reading any more messages until I know what I'm doing. If I'm not letting*

*Woodstock decide for me, I'm surely not allowing
Birdseye to make my choices for me.*

Her ponytail was starting to give her a headache, so
Zoey let her hair down. She ran a brush through her dark
brown tresses before venturing into the hallway. She
didn't feel as though she'd been in her room very long,
but the upper hallway had grown darker.

Before she started down the stairs, she remembered
the box of letters and journals in her closet. Since they
were going to be staying in, it would be a good time to
read more. Jake did seem to enjoy hearing about
Grandma Matilda and Grandpa Joseph nearly as much as
she did. Besides, the alternative was to torture herself
with indecision. With that in mind, she went back for the
box.

Jake was in the living room when she arrived, and
she set the box on the rectangular coffee table.

He sat on the walnut-brown, leather ottoman near
the fire, and used the ladle to dish up bowls of the
steaming hot soup. Dressed in red and black buffalo
flannel pants and a red long-sleeved shirt, he looked so
comfortable there by the fire whipping up their dinner.
She thought back to how they were practically strangers
two weeks ago and how she was not looking forward to

going back to New York and resuming their separate lives.

"It smells good," Zoey said as she joined him by the fireplace.

"I know, I'm salivating over here."

The pot was removed from the fire and resting on the red brick hearth. Like the pot, the two bowls were steaming. "Is it too hot? I could get some ice."

"I'll just blow on mine," Jake said, stirring his bowl with the spoon.

Zoey went for ice and returned in time to see Jake sucking in air and his eyes squinting as he set the bowl down. "Stay right there, and I'll get the sugar."

"Sugar?"

Trying to hurry, Zoey grabbed the little sugar jar used for coffee and a spoon from the kitchen.

"It's pretty hot," he said. "What's the sugar for?"

"If you put white sugar on a burned tongue, it helps soothe the burn."

He brightened a bit at that, watching as Zoey scooped half a spoonful from the sugar jar.

"Put the sugar right on the places you burned," Zoey said, handing him the spoon.

Jake tipped the spoon so the sugar ran over his

tongue and into his mouth.

"Let it sit on your tongue and dissolve," Zoey advised as she dropped a pair of ice cubes into his bowl and her own. She tried not to look at him since he looked pretty silly with his tongue sticking out covered in sugar, but it was impossible not to smile.

"I see dat," he said, trying to speak while holding his tongue out.

Zoey's grin deepened, and she laughed.

"I don't even care that it looks funny—it's helping." He laughed and then put another spoonful onto his tongue.

The second time around with the sugar, Zoey managed to snap a picture with her phone.

"That's not right," he said, holding his hand out for the phone.

Zoey held it up, showing him the picture. "Oh, come on, it's funny. You have lots of pictures of me. I need to have at least one of you, don't I?"

Jake playfully rolled his eyes and smirked.

Zoey nodded and began eating the cooled soup.

Jake stirred his bowl a little while longer before he tried it again. Zoey winced for him, thinking about how it could hurt if it were still too hot.

"Mmmm, so good," he said, giving her a wink.

"How's your tongue?"

Jake's smile grew. "It's a lot better, and now, it's sweet, too."

"Good, I'm glad." Zoey set aside her empty bowl and unfolded the fluffy Sherpa blanket. "Your Christmas pajamas are sweet, too."

Jake nodded. "My mother gives me a new pair of Christmas pajamas every year—it's a tradition we've had since I was a kid."

Zoey smiled at the idea of Christmas traditions, feeling so grateful to be in the inn that year for the holidays.

"Any chance that box you brought down has the rest of the letters? I'm dying to hear what happens next."

Zoey nodded. "It does."

"What's a guy got to do to get some one-on-one reading time with *the* Zoey Larson?"

She was blushing when she stood to get the box and laughed when she noticed that Jake had moved onto the loveseat next to where she was sitting. "I can read to you this time if you'd rather not. I just love hearing your voice."

"You've got a second bowl of soup, so I'll read first,

smooth talker."

"It's the sugar. I'm usually very jumbled when it comes to asking for what I want."

Zoey laughed outright at that, not even trying to hide how hilarious she found that claim.

"What? I am." He smiled. "I am, I swear."

"Then I must bring out your straight-forward approach."

Jake's shoulders shook as he laughed. "You must."

# CHAPTER 20

**Matilda Dunn's Diary**
**December 23, 1966**

Joseph arrived two hours late at the Victorian, but I'd waited because I knew I'd be just as restless if I went home. His facial features were strained when he first walked in to find me. Joseph's eyes were a little red, and his stance rigid. When he saw me, he smiled—his body relaxing at that moment.

I ran over to him, wanting to punch him in

the shoulder for making me wait and hug him because I was relieved to see him. I hugged him, of course.

He told me about how his parents were livid. His grandparents were called in as well to try and 'talk some sense' into him. Joseph said that he wanted to explain it to his parents calmly. They hadn't listened, and he told me that things escalated quickly.

Joseph has always been so respectful and obedient to his parents. He told me that they were shocked when he raised his voice in response to their raised voices. He was so brave to stand up for himself.

Joseph told them that he was not returning to Stanford. He told them of our dream to build a bed and breakfast. His father said that it was a side business—just a hobby, not a way to make a living. Joseph said his mother cried, and it hurt him to see her cry, but he said that he couldn't give in to them anymore.

They told him that if he wasn't returning to school and was choosing to throw his life away, he couldn't expect to live at home. That was why it took Joseph so long to arrive at the Victorian. He had to pack up his belongings from his room and load them into his car.

I cried for him when I heard his family had thrown him out and told him they didn't want to see him until he was ready to reason. Joseph is so very strong, and I don't know what I'd do if I were in his situation. What's more, Joseph told me not to cry because he is the happiest he's ever been.

He said he's happy because from now on he will make his own decisions. Joseph said that he doesn't care what mistakes he makes from here on out because at least they will be his and not choices forced upon him. I told him how proud I am of him and for the first time since he arrived, he looked afraid, and it surprised me.

I asked him what was wrong. Joseph said

that he'd been hoping that his parents would give him the money they were going to put into school tuition toward starting our dream and our lives together, but his parents refused and told him he was cut off.

I think Joseph was afraid that I wouldn't want to wait to buy the Victorian. Hopefully, I convinced him that earning money together was going to make the Victorian all the more special to us.

Even though Joseph's having to stay with his friend Ernest for the time being, I can't help feeling so very happy that he's back!

**December 25, 1966**

We spent Christmas Eve together. We went caroling with everybody, and we took a sleigh ride just as the sun was setting. Wrapped up in a blanket with Joseph looking at that pink, purple, orange, and deep teal blue sky—Joseph told me that he couldn't wait to spend the rest of his life with me.

He said if he had money to buy me a ring, he would have asked me to marry him right then. I told him that I wished he would ask me because I'd tell him YES! But, true to character, Joseph insisted that it had to be done correctly. Apparently, if there's not a ring being offered and he's not down on one knee, it just can't happen.

I love him. I love him. I truly am so in love with him. So, I'll wait, and even if he offers me a ring that's made from the cheapest metal or even paper, I am going to say yes!

**January 8, 1967**

Things have been so busy since Christmas I haven't had much of a chance to write anything down. I got a new job that pays as much as both of my part-time jobs and even a little bit more. I work at the Billings Ranch. It isn't a glamorous job to most, but I love it. I'm working with the horses and leading guided tours, driving sleighs, and volunteering to help wherever else I can. That's enough to keep me busy, but that's not all. Joseph got a job, too.

Ernest's father runs a building company and the local hardware store. He hired Joseph on full time. We've both been working so hard that there are days we don't see each other. He always calls me to wish me sweet dreams and tell me he loves me.

We hope to save all our money and buy the Victorian. Joseph is finding out who owns the property currently since Marshall Taylor passed away just before the new year. Once we find out who owns it, we will be able to find out how much they want for the place. Joseph was so cute. He said he's going to bargain and make sure we get a fair price. How could I not love that man?

**March 3, 1967**

Joseph's grandfather approached him at work last night and told him to come to his house for a talk. Joseph agreed to go, and he did. He called me this morning before work and told me not to worry, but that his grandfather wanted to find out just how serious Joseph is about the path he's chosen.

He said that his grandfather didn't like it

but that he understood and best of all, he respected Joseph for being his own man. I think that meant a lot to Joseph. I was happy it went well for him.

When I got off work, I was surprised to see Joseph was there to give me a ride home. I thought he was working late. He said that we'd both been working hard, and we deserved a little celebrating. So, he drove me home so I could shower and change.

When he came by to get me, I was elated to see him dressed so sharp in his navy-blue suit. No one can wear a suit like my Joseph. He looks as good as any man in uniform. Better, even. I don't think I retained a single word Joseph said for the first five minutes after I saw him looking so devilishly handsome.

We went to dinner, and then we went to the Victorian. He'd put up Christmas lights in the backyard. He plugged them in and turned on a radio with a tape of music he'd recorded for us.

We danced under the full moon in the light of the white strung lights all around us like swirling stardust. I didn't think anything could make the night more magical than that.

But then, Joseph got down on one knee and stole my breath away. He presented me with a beautiful ring that belonged to his great-grandmother and asked me to be his wife! I cried even though I tried so hard not to. I said yes, and he kissed me, and we danced to "Just One Look" by Doris Troy, "My Girl" by the Temptations, and "With This Ring" by The Platters.

I'll never ever forget this magically perfect day.

### April 14, 1967

We are planning to get married at the end of the month. Everything is just falling into place, and I can't believe it. Mom let me try on her wedding dress, and it fit like it was made just for me. I can't wait until Joseph sees me in it!

We'll be married in the Universalist Church. Luckily, Mom is good friends with the minister's wife. It will be an intimate, small ceremony. My parents aren't wealthy like Joseph's, but they offered to provide food for the reception. I know it will be a sacrifice for them, but I feel so loved that they want to do this for Joseph and me.

The hardest part of all of this is, of course, Joseph's parents. Joseph and I went to their home to invite them to the wedding, but they wouldn't see us. Joseph gave the invitation to the maid to give to his parents. I know it hurts him that they are still closing him out.

When we were walking back down the path to the road, Joseph hugged me close to his side and said, "No matter what they do, it doesn't change how much I love you."

He is the only man I will ever love.

**May 3, 1967**

Most of April was a whirlwind of preparing for the wedding. Maybell was my maid of honor. Ernest and Ricky were the best men for Joseph, who refused to choose between the two. His grandparents told him they would be there, but we didn't hear from Joseph's parents or his older brother.

I didn't sleep the night before the wedding. I was so excited and nervous. There were so

many nights in April that I spent praying that
Joseph's parents would come to the wedding or
at least tell Joseph if they weren't so that he
could settle that matter and not have to wonder
and hope.

Before I walked down the aisle to meet the
only man in the world I'll ever love, I asked
Maybell and Mom to check and see if Joseph's
parents arrived at least a dozen times. When it
was time to walk, and they still had not come, I'll
admit it made me so angry for Joseph.

I expected to see the sadness in his eyes
when I started down the aisle. There wasn't
anything in his eyes or on his face but joy and
affection. After I repeated the vows the
minister told me to repeat, I asked him if I
could add a few of my own, though I didn't wait
for him to answer. I promised Joseph that I
would never abandon him, that I would never
leave his side, and that he could always count on
me loving him.

Joseph repeated the vows of the minister and then promised me that he would spend every day making sure I knew how much he loved me and working hard to make our dreams come true. It was so beautiful.

Then at the reception, Joseph's grandfather surprised us by giving us his cabin in Waterbury, so we'd have a home of our own. He also gave us some money. He said it was to start our life off right, and it was just enough when combined with what we'd saved to buy the Victorian!

Instead of leaving for our honeymoon as we'd initially planned, we went to speak with Robert Taylor, the man who'd inherited the land and Victorian. He said that he'd only charge us for the land because the house was liable to be condemned. We paid $11,326... and the Victorian is ours!

We plan to live in Waterbury and work to repair the Victorian and make it into a bed and breakfast.

Last night, when we were cleaning the Victorian, a spring rainstorm broke out. It was coming down so hard we decided to stay the night in the Victorian.

The thunder was so loud it was shaking the house, and I couldn't get it out of my head how Mr. Taylor said the house should be condemned. What if the storm toppled the house? Of course, now that it's daylight that thought seems silly, but the house honestly was shaking. That thunder was right on top of us.

Joseph must have noticed my tossing and turning. He started telling me about an inn on the way up to Stanford called Barn Owl Inn. He laughed when I told him that sounded like a haunted place to stay, even though he agreed with me that it did. Pretty soon, I was laughing, too, and I forgot all about being afraid of the Victorian shaking apart into a pile of wood.

Joseph asked me what we should call our bed and breakfast. I suppose I'd always thought we'd call it The Victorian. Only last night, when we were laughing and talking about what an impression a name could make, I realized The Victorian wouldn't reflect what kind of place we wanted it to be.

I told him it should be something meaningful for us. I had been thinking about this name for a while, and I was so excited to share my thoughts with Joseph finally. One of the first things I remember noticing about the Victorian was the abundance of snapdragon flowers growing along the wraparound porch. A few weeks ago, I came across a book called The Folklore of Flowers. I decided to sift through the pages and learn a bit more about the snapdragon flower.

The moment I began reading, I knew.

I learned that snapdragons stand for grace, and since they often grow in rocky areas— strength. As I explained this to Joseph, he smiled at me in that way that makes me melt.

I knew that he got the symbolism that struck me so profoundly, too. We made it through our rocky times with grace and strength, and the Victorian is the next chapter of our lives together officially as husband and wife.

I knew we had come up with the perfect name of the place where we will surely live out our dreams. As soon as I heard it, I knew it was right. No, not merely right, but perfect.

The Snapdragon Inn.

# CHAPTER 21

"Wow," Zoey said as she lowered the journal.

Jake nodded in agreement. "I know I never got to meet Grandma Matilda, but I love her for writing all this down and for saving Joseph's letters. She left you a full, complete picture, and it's so meaningful."

"I know. I mean, I always knew this place was important to Grandma, but it wasn't just important to her... it's a part of her, and it's a part of me, too." A big fat tear trailed down her cheek, and she quickly swiped it away. "I've been so selfish. How could I even think of not keeping the Snapdragon?"

"You weren't selfish, Zoey. You wanted to keep a

job that you love."

Zoey bit her lower lip and wrinkled her nose. "Mmm, maybe not love. I mean, I love writing and getting paid to write, but the office politics? I could really do without them. Well, I do love getting to collaborate with other writers and the recognition of getting to work for a place with status like Birdseye Publishing."

Jake nodded slowly. "You know, you remind me a lot of your Grandpa Joseph. You are a cautious person, and there's nothing wrong with that. But…" Suddenly, his cheeks flushed, and he shook his head. "I should really shut up. You don't need to hear my advice."

"I want to hear what you were going to say. Don't stop now, Jake."

"It's not my place to say anything, really."

Zoey set the journal she was still holding on the end table next to the couch and then swung her legs up over his lap. "I'm not letting you up until you tell me, so you might as well give in now."

He looked down at her legs draped over his lap and laughed. "I can honestly say I didn't expect that reaction from you."

"You're my friend. I want to know what you think,

Jake. I respect your opinion."

Jake set his hands on her shins, and even though there was a blanket between her legs and his hands, she still felt the heat of them radiating through. "Okay, I don't know if it's going to help you. All I was going to say is that maybe since you are looking at your options so cautiously, you're not seeing all of them."

"Not seeing all of them? I can see that I can sell the inn to the town, or I can give up my job and run it. Is there another option that I'm not considering?"

"Well, you see it in an all or nothing sort of way. You said you love writing and collaborating with other writers. What's to stop you from writing from here and collaborating with the writers you've already got in your network? You can still collaborate through Facetime or Skype, right?"

Zoey tilted her head to the side as she considered the idea. "I could a little, I suppose, but not in the same way I do now. I'm not around to go dive into the latest scandals or do the footwork and interview people face to face since that's not the kind of news that happens out here."

"True. You could write historical features and take your time with them since you'd be your own boss. That way, you could schedule in travel time at your leisure. Or," he said, his grin widening, "you could try your hand at fiction."

"I could, but I like your historical features idea much better. I mean, there is tons of history right here in this town and in the surrounding towns, too. Only where am I going to publish? Birdseye wouldn't allow me to contribute to them periodically."

Jake made a gesture with his hand that seemed to encompass everywhere around them. "Where can't you publish? This is the digital age, Zoey. You've got a great resume already in place, and you've got a talent for writing historical features. I read the article you wrote on The Old Stone House. The one where the Battle of Brooklyn was waged. I didn't know that place existed, and even if I had, I would not have been interested in going there based on its name. But," Jake said, holding up a finger, "I had to go after you brought that place to life in your article."

"Really?"

"Yes, really. It's one of the reasons I was hoping you'd write about this place. Something about the way you see places has me captivated. I'll always want to read your stuff."

A Winter in Woodstock

Zoey felt her cheeks heating. "You're too nice to me, Jake. Thank you, I appreciate you saying that, and I do think you have a point. What's to stop me from writing after I get this place back in action?"

"Not a thing."

"Oh, my gosh, you're so right. I'm doing it. I'm keeping the Snapdragon!" Leaning forward, she took Jake by surprise, hugging him tight and kissing his cheek. "Thank you."

His face turned toward her immediately after she kissed his cheek and his lips were so close to hers, she could almost feel them. Fear swept through her, and she backed up before she couldn't stop herself.

Fear of rejection was something she hadn't entirely conquered after trying so many times to get her parents to care about her. It sure was an inconvenient time for that particular weakness to stick its ugly head out.

"I'm going to text Kenzie and Celeste back right now and tell them to offer the job to someone else. They gave me a deadline to get word to them either way by midnight tonight. Now that I know what I'm going to do, I'll get this off my plate. Right? Right."

*And now I'm babbling.*

"I'm glad you know what you want to do now. It's

great to see you smiling again. I'm going to miss it. Almost want to kick my butt for pointing out that you could have the best of both worlds."

Zoey wasn't surprised when she heard her grandma's voice telling her, *"Don't ever stop trying. Sometimes putting yourself out there hurts, but you'll never regret trying. What you will regret, my dear, is being too afraid to try."* She stared at his hands still draped over her shins.

Grandma Matilda had been talking about Zoey trying to build a relationship with her parents, but what she'd said applied to her current condition of fear just as much.

Raising her gaze from his callused hands, her brown eyes inched up his arms until she looked into his vivid green eyes. "I… I'm not good at this kind of thing."

"What kind of thing?" His voice was so warm it jolted her. "Being admired? Liked?"

"I'm not good at opening up and letting anyone close to me."

He nodded, his eyes heating up as they continued to look into hers. "I know."

"I'd like to get better at it," Zoey admitted, trying to pretend she didn't feel the way her face was burning or the drumroll her heartbeat was pounding out in her chest.

"With anyone in particular? Don't say Corey Finch."

Zoey laughed, and Jake took that opportunity to pull on her legs and slide her closer to him so that when he claimed her lips with his, he could hold her close. Taking the lead with such assertive action gave no room for her fear to linger.

She was wrapped in warmth and encircled by his arms—the arms of a man who cared enough to help her through one of the hardest decisions she ever had to make. He cared about her enough not to broach the subject of their mutual attraction until she was ready. He cared enough to resolve things with her after she lost her temper so badly.

In so many ways, Jake had been telling her ever since they arrived in Woodstock that he cared about her, but she'd been too blind or too scared to see it.

At that moment, she decided to break down her walls.

She returned the embrace, feeling shocked at how right it felt to be held by Jake.

# CHAPTER 22

**Six Months Later**

"Are you getting in?" Jake asked Zoey as she posed by the basket attached to the red, blue, and yellow hot air balloon.

"Um, in the basket?" Zoey wrinkled her nose as she flashed her teeth in a nervous smile. "I wasn't planning on it."

Jake snapped another picture and then handed his camera to Gertrude. "Can you take one of us?"

"I was just going to suggest it." Gertrude smiled, raising it before Jake even had a chance to get next to Zoey. He dashed to Zoey as she turned toward him with a bright and eager smile.

Jake wrapped his arms around her waist as hers slid over his shoulders. They smiled for the camera and Gertrude took the picture but insisted they needed several angles.

"We've got the Snapdragon Inn completely repaired and our first set of guests checked in. Maybell's there to watch over things, and I think this is the perfect way to celebrate." Jake said.

"I thought this was the perfect feature for your blog?" Zoey teased.

Jake nuzzled her soft cheek with his lips and nose. "Can't it be both?"

Zoey looked up at the large, colorful balloon and let out a shaky breath. "It's not scary to you to climb into that little basket and count on a balloon to carry us through the sky?"

"Maybe a little scary, but mostly, it's going to be exciting, thrilling, and what's more, it is going to give us a killer view of the Snapdragon."

"An aerial shot of the inn? That's a brilliant idea!" Zoey kissed him, and he held on.

Gertrude was snapping pictures like she was firing a machine gun instead of a camera. They would have photos for days of that kiss, but neither of them minded.

"All aboard," Herman announced from inside the basket. "Who's ready to climb into the sky?"

"Are we sure about this?" Zoey asked as Jake stepped back.

He kissed both of her hands and then signaled Gertrude to return the camera. "I am. I've always wanted to try this, but you don't have to, Zoey. I'll get the picture of the Snapdragon."

"No, I don't just want to see the picture. I'm coming. I want to see it myself." Zoey took hold of one of the ropes and climbed into the basket. "Don't crash us into anything, Herman."

"Don't worry. I only shake up the ride for the tourists. You two locals can count on smooth as whipped cream sailing."

"Whipped cream, huh?" Jake laughed as he climbed into the basket with his camera.

Herman grinned extra big, which Jake and Zoey both noticed he did when someone asked him about some of his more peculiar choice of word selection. "Yep, that's right. Ya see, whipped cream looks like the puffy clouds, and it isn't the same as taking a ship out to sea."

"That's all true," Jake said, sharing a smile with

Zoey.

"You know, I don't think there is anyone else who could talk me into getting into this basket that's about to propel into the sky," Zoey said, giving Jake a poke to the ribs.

Gertrude waved to them as she backed up. "Have a lovely time."

"Bye, Gertrude, see you in a little while."

Herman shouted out a sound that was probably meant to sound like a cowboy but was more like a war cry. Jake held her hand as the basket lifted off the ground.

"We're due for a bit of a bump here," Herman said just before it hit. "We're still tied down, and I'm just gonna fire up our balloon nice and hot, then we'll pull that line and be off."

"I'm so glad you talked me into this," Zoey said, squeezing Jake's hand.

"Are you sure? We're not quite going yet."

Zoey smiled at him. "Yeah, I just wanted to make sure to say thank you now in case I forget when we're up higher in the sky. It's so easy to get overwhelmed with all that's going on and forget to tell you thank you. I mean, these past six months have been some of the best months of my life. I'm so happy, and you're a huge part of that, Jake."

"Oh, boy, Jake. What are you going to say to that? That's a hard act to follow," Herman put in. "Speaking of thanking you, Jake. Your blog has up and doubled business for Woodstock. Lots of folks are calling your blog and Zoey's Snapdragon Inn the second Woodstock boom."

Zoey's smile grew with delight. "That makes me so happy."

"Then it's a good time to pull on that rope and set us free. Who wants to do the honor?" Herman asked and let out another loud, "Yahoo!"

"Give it a pull, Zoey," Jake said and snapped another picture as she took hold of the rope.

Zoey bit her lower lip as she looked down below at the people gathered to watch the hot air balloon launch. "Pull it with me?"

"Let's do it," Jake said, taking hold of the rope just under her grip. They pulled, and the balloon soared upward.

Jake put his arms around her as she let out an excited squeal.

"I can't believe we're doing this!" she cried.

The crowd below cheered and continued cheering as the other hot air balloons joined them in the sky.

"This is unbelievable. Look at those geese." Jake pointed to the flying arrow formation. "Feels like we're flying, too."

"It does. It's incredible."

Jake lifted his camera, snapping pictures of the view of the hot air balloons rising to join them, and the geese.

Herman turned up the heat, and they soared higher into the sky. The wind was light but grew stronger the higher they climbed, setting them on their path to sail over Woodstock and some of the other neighboring towns.

"I see it," Zoey said, her heart swelling with joy at the sight of the Snapdragon from the sky. "The new roof looks great, doesn't it?"

"It looks like paradise nestled in the Garden of Eden, is what it looks like," Jake said, taking more pictures. "You were so right about that garden maze in the back. It's beautiful even from up here."

Zoey nodded. "It really is."

"You two have done Matilda's inn justice. She's shining brighter than ever before," Herman agreed, leaning toward them and making the basket tip forward a bit.

"Thanks," Jake said, moving to rebalance the craft.

Herman laughed at Jake's effort. "You're a nervous one, aren't you? Don't worry, we've got sandbags keeping up from keeling over."

"You're a fearless devil, aren't you, Herman?" Jake asked with a laugh.

"So are you," Zoey said to Jake. "You've traveled all over the world and led such a rich and exciting life. I keep wondering, are you really happy here with me in Woodstock?"

Jake gestured for Herman to move so he could draw closer to Zoey again without tipping the basket. He slid his arms around her waist, looking at the Snapdragon Inn over her shoulder, with her back pressed against his chest. "Every day with you is an adventure, Zoey. I wouldn't miss it for the world."

THE END

Made in the USA
Coppell, TX
04 April 2020

18426664R00132